Sweet & Spicy SPELLS

CHRISTINE D'ABO
RENEE FIELD

ELLORA'S CAVE
ROMANTICA PUBLISHING

An Ellora's Cave Romantica Publication

www.ellorascave.com

Sweet and Spicy Spells

ISBN 9781419961229
ALL RIGHTS RESERVED.
Sweet and Spicy Spells Copyright © 2007 Chistine d'Abo & Renee Field
Edited by Briana St. James.
Cover art by Photography and cover art by Les Byerley.

Electronic book publication October 2007
Trade paperback publication 2010

With the exception of quotes used in reviews, this book may not be reproduced or used in whole or in part by any means existing without written permission from the publisher, Ellora's Cave Publishing, Inc.® 1056 Home Avenue, Akron OH 44310-3502.

Warning: The unauthorized reproduction or distribution of this copyrighted work is illegal. Criminal copyright infringement, including infringement without monetary gain, is investigated by the FBI and is punishable by up to 5 years in federal prison and a fine of $250,000.
(http://www.fbi.gov/ipr/)

This book is a work of fiction and any resemblance to persons, living or dead, or places, events or locales is purely coincidental. The characters are productions of the author's imagination and used fictitiously.

SWEET AND SPICY SPELLS

ಙ

Sweet and Spicy Spells

Chapter One

ജ

"Sex."

"What?" sputtered Kisha Morgan, rising naked from the bathtub, dripping white sudsy bubbles onto the wooden floor. "Come again?"

"That's your problem, sis. You probably haven't come in what...a year? Sex, most definitely, that's what you need. And lots of it. I'm thinking hot steamy sex. That's your magic pill that will make it all click."

Kisha grabbed a black towel and quickly dried off. She draped it around herself but didn't say anything to her older, much more experienced sister. She snapped her fingers, hoping she'd end up with clothes. *Damn.* She was once again in the bath, knee-deep in the vanilla-scented bubbles.

"See, that's what I mean. Sex will relax you, make all those instinctive muscles in your brain work. Better yet, it will make them mesh together. Trust me, you need sex." Her sister actually snapped her own fingers to emphasize her point.

"Shut up, Priscilla. I can work my magic when I really need it," she replied indignantly. She huffed and rose once again, this time walking dripping wet from the bathroom, down the long drafty hall to her bedroom. Her nipples puckered from the cool air. She ached to snap her fingers and magically become warm and dressed, but no way was she going to have a repeat performance and end up sputtering bubbles again in the tub.

"Witches were made for sex," chanted Priscilla as she materialized elegantly on Kisha's bed, dressed to kill. Tight black leather skirt, knee-high heeled boots, a black leather corset she wore like a shirt to better outline her well-endowed

7

Christine d'Abo & Renee Field

chest and long, straight midnight hair trailed over her shoulders. At six feet, Priscilla was the complete package. Sexy as sin. The perfect witch.

"Are you listening to me? Witches were made for sex. And it's not like you haven't had sex before. You're sooo not a virgin, so don't get all frosty with me."

Kisha picked up a nearby pillow and threw it at her sister. She watched as her sister blinked and the pillow neatly disappeared. *Nice trick,* Kisha thought.

"Like you said, I've had sex. It didn't help, so there."

"You know, anyone can have sex, Kis. He's gotta make you come, big time, to make it really count."

Kis. Her sister hadn't used her pet nickname in years. The last time she'd heard that name was a good ten years ago when Priscilla had been the one to inform her that their parents had been killed in a car accident during a freak snowstorm.

Goose bumps formed along Kisha's skin. *Is something up? Something big?* She wondered why Priscilla had appeared now. Six months ago, Kisha had practically begged for her to come for a visit to help restore the old family farmhouse. The farmhouse had been left to them by Alice Morgan, their last great-aunt, who had taken them in after their parents' deaths. Her sister had told Kisha in no uncertain terms what she thought of the old farmhouse—pile of rubbish.

The farmhouse had always been a comforting place for Kisha. Ten years ago it had needed work. Today it practically screamed for an extreme makeover team to tear out every wall. But that had always been the charm of the place. Their aunt had lived her life with magic. Hence, the farmhouse had no electrical wiring and the plumbing, well, that was another matter entirely. Kisha was at least grateful her sister hadn't shown up a half hour earlier when she'd fought spell after spell to get the ancient claw-toed bathtub to fill up with hot, not cold water.

8

Sweet and Spicy Spells

That sense of family magic and even the scent of freshly baked cookies permeated the aura of the farmhouse and she was determined to restore it. It had always been her place of refuge, even before her parents' sudden deaths. And after living for the last five years in the heart of the city, surrounded by concrete buildings, the stench of garbage and the mass of people at all hours of the day, the lure of the old farmhouse was what had driven her back after her great-aunt's death.

Mind you, Priscilla had a point. She really had to get her magic working. Witches were made for sex, she'd give her sister that. But she'd had lots of sex. Lots of men and nothing. Not even a glimmer of a tingle to bring her over that edge. Sadly, the only thing that made her come was herself. Her fingers, her fantasy and voilà! She could fly over that mountain.

Kisha realized her sister was still talking, so she quickly shelved her fantasy dream man away. Maybe tonight she'd let her fingers come out to play, pretending it was him. The thought sent a shiver of anticipation spiraling through her still cold body.

"You need to be more assertive. Tell him what works." Priscilla paused. "You do know what works, right, Kis?"

Kisha moved to the old armoire and grabbed a bright pink hair scrunchy. She wrung out more water from her still wet hair and then tied it back into a tight ponytail. "I'm not a kid anymore, sis. I think I've figured out what works for me by now."

Priscilla moved off the bed. "Really, that's good to know, because here I was thinking *you* were the cold bitch instead of me."

"You know, Priscilla, I've never thought of you like that," said Kisha.

"I know you don't, but others do. I'm not stupid. I know what they say about me. But it's okay…really. I know exactly

9

what I am. I'm the best witch in the Northern Hemisphere and I intend to keep it that way. So back to your little problem."

Little problem? Try ever-since-I-was-born problem. My spells have never really worked when I've needed them. Kisha fought not to groan. *What will it take to make my sister leave me alone?* Kisha gulped. Agreeing to her terms because she never backs down.

Kisha realized then that she was the complete opposite to her sister. She didn't look one bit witchy except for her fiery orange hair, which didn't have a hint of auburn in it, more carrot-hued than anything else. She was petite, reaching five feet on a good day. She tried for elegance but usually ended up looking childish and clumsy.

"Two days," said Priscilla. "Here, let me help."

Two days? For what?

Kisha nodded a yes, once again giving in to her sister. Her sister conjured up a blood red shirt, cut too low for Kisha's liking, tight blue jeans and the same high-heeled boots Priscilla wore, only Kisha's now matched the color of the shockingly low-cut shirt, which caused her breasts to almost spill over the top. She peeked inside. Yup, her sister had even conjured up a black lace underwire bra, which caused her breasts to swell even more.

"I'll bite, two days for what?" asked Kisha, stumbling as she took a step in the too-tall boots, readjusting her breasts. Breasts that always made her feel uncomfortable. They were too large for her liking. It was the one trait her sister said made her a man magnet. *As if! And so what?* None of the men who landed in her bed could beat her fantasy lover.

"Two days until All Hallow's Eve. Forty-eight hours for you to perfect your magic. That's what I came to tell you in the first place. But like everything in this godforsaken dump, I got sidetracked. Tell me again why you want to fix this pile of rubble…no, on second thought, don't. That's the last thing I need to hear."

Sweet and Spicy Spells

Kisha gulped. "Two days, you can't be serious. I'm sure you're mistaken."

"Sadly, I'm not. Two days and you have to perform the ritual before the Archana Council Elders. That's why I've resorted to desperate measures—"

"Desperate measures? Please tell me you haven't done anything stupid. I really can fix this myself," said Kisha, picking up the wet towel to drape it across the old wicker rocker in the corner of the room.

Her sister zapped the towel from the rocker and suspended it magically in midair. "So fix this."

Kisha pursed her lips together. *I can do this. I will do this. I'll show her and then she'll leave me alone in peace so I can get back to restoring the farmhouse.*

"See, you can't do it, Kis," tsked her sister.

"I'm just thinking," replied Kisha, sorting all the magical spells she knew in her head until she thought she'd found the one.

"Like I said. That's your problem. You think too much. You need to simply let the magic flow from your subconscious and believe in it."

Kisha grinned. She'd found it. She closed her eyes and spewed forth the words with glee.

Her sister's laughter caused her to open her eyes. She audibly groaned. *So much for getting it right.* Instead of making the towel float back to the rocker she'd turned it into a bar of soap. *Soap! How in the hell did I end up with soap? I told it to float, not soap.* She shook her head in frustration.

"Like I said, you need to get laid and come like there ain't no tomorrow. So I've taken it upon myself to arrange—"

"Oh my spells, don't tell me you've fixed me up? Do you remember what happened the last time you tried something like that?" said Kisha.

Christine d'Abo & Renee Field

"That was with a mortal. And he really did deserve to be turned into a toad. I had no idea he would try *that* with you, Kis. But don't worry. It's all been taken care of," said her sister.

There was a strange gleam in her sister's eye that terrified Kisha. "That's exactly what I'm afraid of," she mumbled.

"Well, don't be. You are in your big sister's capable hands. Ahh, I do believe he's here," announced Priscilla, a moment before a black mist covered the bedroom.

When it finally settled and no one had appeared, Kisha laughed. "Look who's losing their touch," she giggled.

"Ooh, that is *so* not funny. He's going to pay big time for this joke," muttered Priscilla and then, with a poof, she was gone.

What Priscilla hadn't noticed was the large sleek black housecat that jumped down from the window ledge, blinked its emerald almond-shaped eyes at Kisha and meowed.

"So much for my man," muttered Kisha. She immediately yanked off the high-heeled boots to replace them with her sturdy, practical white sneakers.

* * * * *

Foster was furious with his brother Zack. There was no way he was going to meekly agree to the assignment his brother had thrown his way. He wasn't an apprentice warlock anymore, looking to simply please his older sibling. He was a warlock to be reckoned with in his own right.

But instead of yelling at each other, Zack had talked him into a warlock fight. Now the two of them were casting one magical spell after another inside the glass-covered courtyard of their home, Colard Castle.

"I am not going to do it," said Foster. "I don't care what you promised that witch." He punctuated his words by zapping right and left at his brother, willing the electrical bolts to hit their mark.

Sweet and Spicy Spells

"Like I said, you don't have a choice. *Relevo!*" replied Zack, smoothly moving out of the way.

Foster hated his brother's arrogant tone. It was the one thing he didn't like about his eighteen-months-older sibling. Well, one of many things, he thought, forcing his attention back as Zack leveled a zap directly at his head.

Pay attention, little brother, said Zack inside Foster's head.

"Cut that out!" shouted Foster. *I hate when he does that and he knows it.*

"Then get with the program. You're going to fuck her, so let's end this here and now!" said Zack.

The other ten warlocks who were currently residing at Colard Castle were placing bets on who would win. Both brothers knew it. A part of them actually enjoyed it, but neither would admit that.

"It's not like you to pass up sex, Foster. I promised Priscilla you'd have sex with her sister. Fuck, man, have you seen Prissy? She's the hottest bitch...I mean witch this side of the state," said Zack.

Even as his brother spewed forth his monologue, Foster had to duck to his right to avoid the fast zaps his brother aimed at him. *I think he's enjoying this way too much.*

Foster fought not to groan. Sure he'd seen Prissy, what warlock hadn't? Sex oozed out of every pore of that witch's body, but strangely his cock barely twitched. He was sick and tired of witches. They all looked the same, identical chocolate chip cookies in a pre-packaged bag, with no substance. Not that he was looking for something more, but he'd give his right ball for something unique, something that actually fired his cock straight up, and yup, he'd like it to be served with chocolate.

"I said. I. Don't. Want. To. Ahh, fuck," mumbled Foster, bowing his head, admitting his defeat to his brother, who had nicked his shoulder. First cut was first cut, no matter how frigging small.

13

Christine d'Abo & Renee Field

Like I said, fuck that witch silly, brother. And brother dear, her name is Kisha.

Those taunting words said privately irritated him more than losing, and what type of witch name was Kisha, wondered Foster.

Then, poof, Foster was blinking up at one dazzling tiny woman whose bright orange hair caught the strands of the sun, making it appear alive and tantalizing as it swished like a cat's tail in a tight ponytail. He inhaled the scent of vanilla soap and he could have sworn he smelled freshly baked chocolate chip cookies — it was the scent of heaven and sex and his cock knew it. Plus she had an ass to quite literally die for, he thought as she bent over to yank sinfully high boots off, providing him with a perfect view of her curvaceous form clad in tight jeans.

"Well well well, who knew I'd enjoy losing this much," he muttered as he transformed from a housecat back into his wizard form.

Sweet and Spicy Spells

Chapter Two

ஐ

Priscilla zapped smack into the middle of Harry's Hideout in a cloud of red smoke that only she could produce and began to scan the bar for that low-life, double-crossing, pain-in-the-ass Zack Kane. A waiter appeared beside Priscilla with her Blue Lagoon and a smile on his face. She loved being the Cauldron Cup champ and all the privileges that went with the title. And she had no intention of that changing anytime soon, despite all the rumors she'd heard to the contrary this past week.

"Kane. Where is he?" she asked the young man as she swallowed a large gulp of her drink. Shit, she couldn't remember the waiter's name for the life of her, despite the fact he always had her drink waiting. Kisha was the one who was good at details. While Priscilla wished she was here, hopefully Kisha would soon be getting fucked so hard the magic would pound back into her. And for once in her life, Priscilla wouldn't feel like she'd let her little sister down.

Thankfully, the young waiter didn't seem to mind her lack of pleasantries and gestured with his chin toward a dimly lit corner of the bar.

"Mr. Kane is in the lounge. It's by invitation only up there, Ms. Morgan. I'm not sure if you can get past the spell security."

Priscilla smiled and winked seductively at the man. She had to fight the urge to chuckle when he blushed and found something really interesting to look at on the floor. She'd been looking for Zack and didn't appreciate being sent on a wild goose chase. The wizards at Colard Castle told her she'd just missed him when she'd shown up. Some of them were still

15

Christine d'Abo & Renee Field

bitching about losing a bet. Never a good sign when the brothers Kane were having a tiff.

And how the hell did he manage to cast a spell in Harry's anyway? The last time she'd forgotten and cast a minor one, they'd almost threatened to revoke her free pass to the bar, Cauldron Cup champion or not.

"Getting into trouble is something I'm good at." She turned and placed a kiss on his cheek, trying not to giggle when he sucked in a deep breath. "You're a peach. Here's a little something for you," and she dropped a bag of herbs that were guaranteed to get him laid on the tray.

When he saw what she'd given him, his blush deepened even more. "Th-thanks. Good luck in the Cup this year." His voice rose several notes as he spoke.

"Luck has nothing to do with it." Priscilla winked again and turned to face the direction of the lounge.

Zack Kane. *Shit.* Priscilla couldn't believe her heart was pounding a little bit faster at the idea of seeing him again. Especially considering what he'd done to her last time they'd met. Pushing away her schoolgirl infatuation, Priscilla took a deep breath and calmed her nerves. She was a much stronger witch and woman than she'd been five years ago. And she had no intention of letting Zack anywhere near her heart. Thank the goddess she'd only been corresponding with him through a messenger spell over the past week. But now it was time to meet up and talk about his plan for helping Kisha. There was also the matter of a little payback for the black mist back at the farmhouse. *So not cool.*

Priscilla sucked down another gulp of her Blue Lagoon before letting her sexiest smile slide onto her face and sauntered across the main bar to the stairs that led up to the lounge. As she walked, she could hear the whispers and whistles of the wizards she passed. It drove them nuts that she could come in here anytime she wanted, throwing all the rules in their collective faces. *Damn fucking straight.* And she wasn't about to stop. Five years running. She was the longest reigning

Sweet and Spicy Spells

champ for the Cauldron Cup and she knew every man in this room wanted to see her lose almost as much as they wanted to fuck her.

Not that either was going to happen any time soon.

As she walked up the stairs, she could feel the build-up of electricity in the air, a tell-tale sign that a wizard of great power was nearby. The security spell snagged her for a moment, slowing her progress before it popped and she was allowed to pass. While the rivalry between witches and warlocks was still strong, they'd learned to overcome their biases over the years. But their powers came from far different places and each could always sense the strangeness of the other.

And Priscilla knew the tingle that was currently caressing every inch of her body. Knew that only a wizard as strong as Zack could provoke this type of reaction in her. It pricked along her skin with each step she took closer to its source. Her body warmed and tingled in all the wrong places. Her neck, her breasts, her cunt all felt like someone was softly caressing them—probably Zack. There was a time she would have willingly thrown herself at his feet and begged him to rip her clothes off, throw her up against the wall and fuck her where she stood. *No!* She was over him, had been for ages.

He doesn't mean a thing to me.

Despite her powers, she couldn't force her eyes to adjust to the darkness of the private lounge. She could tell he was there and alone. She just couldn't see him. The bastard had cast a conceal spell.

"I don't believe my eyes," Zack's rich, baritone voice drifted out from the middle of nowhere. "They'll let anyone into Harry's now."

"It's not my fault the Wizards added the clause that the champion gets free drinks as long as they hold the top prize," she said with a shrug. Sick of the dark, Priscilla snapped her fingers and broke the conceal spell with little effort.

Christine d'Abo & Renee Field

Zack was lounging on the leather couch, a scotch glass in one hand and one of the oldest-looking books she'd ever seen in the other. He looked incredibly relaxed, lying there with one leg stretched out and the other bent, resting against the back of the couch. Priscilla felt the sting of mixed emotions nibble at her bravado, threatening to undermine her carefully constructed confidence.

He made a low tsking noise. "No spell casting in Harry's, Prissy. You may get a spanking for that one."

"What's good for the goose, Zack," she said coolly and rolled her eyes.

"I play by my own rules. Besides, there isn't a wizard here stupid enough to argue with me."

"Thankfully, I'm a witch."

Priscilla let her eyes wander over his body, taking in every detail. Despite the passage of time, his appearance really hadn't changed much in the past five years. He wore his dark blue shirt unbuttoned at the collar with his sleeves rolled halfway up his forearms. She could see the black hairs that covered his chest peeking from beneath his shirt and she couldn't help but wonder what the hell he'd look like naked. His shoulder-length black hair held a tinge of gray around his temples, making him look more sophisticated and, if possible, more handsome than before.

She'd been so in love with him five years ago she hadn't wanted to rush to his bed. Instead, she teased and drew out their relationship, wanting more than just a quick fuck. When he'd walked out of her life with little more than a *see you later*, all thoughts of romantic love went with him. Now all she wanted from him was a good hard fuck.

"So do I meet the high standards of the Cauldron Queen?"

Her gaze immediately shot to his sinfully brown eyes and she could see the laughter there. *Damn arrogant wizard.* He'd always known her buttons. But Priscilla wasn't about to let

18

Sweet and Spicy Spells

him get to her. She did what she always did when she felt threatened — retaliated with sex.

She brought her drink to her lips and, a moment before taking a sip, her tongue darted out and she licked the rim of the glass. It only took a blink to have the cherry that was floating in the blue alcohol rise into the air and over to her lips. She sucked on the cherry as it rested suspended in the air before biting down on the sweet fruit.

"Long time no see, Zack. So what rock have you been hiding under for the past five years?"

Zack's gaze was locked on her mouth and Priscilla couldn't stop her smile. Tired of the taunting, she broke the silent standoff between them and sauntered over to the chair closest to where he lay. The angle of the seat forced her to recline, pushing her corset-covered breasts high into the air. She had to cross her legs to keep from giving Zack too much of a show. Fucking came naturally to her, she was a witch after all, but she wasn't about to send love-them-and-leave-them Zack an invitation. He'd lost that right five years ago.

For his part, Zack managed to keep his relaxed posture. He flipped his book closed and tossed it to the end of the couch. "I've been here and there. I've heard you've been busy."

He punctuated his statement by a lengthy examination of her legs. Priscilla didn't squirm under his intense gaze. It would take more than a little ogling on his part to scare her away.

"*Incomitatus*," he whispered with a wave of his hand and a bubble of nothingness encased them. "Now we can talk without half the bar listening in."

"Ah, but it's more entertaining with an audience," she said and gave him her best pout.

"Why are you here, Prissy? Couldn't find any small animals to harass?"

19

A sudden rage at the use of his nickname for her sent a blast of energy from her, knocking his drink to the floor. "Kisha's the animal lover. I'm here because you didn't answer my last message about who you were sending to help Kisha with her…problem. That and your little trick with the black fog back at Kisha's place."

"How is the old place? I heard it was getting pretty run-down since Kisha can't cast up a hammer and nails to fix it."

"Zack!"

His lips tightened into a thin line and his brow furrowed for a moment before he cocked his head to the side and shot her a lop-sided grin. That heated look sent a jolt through her body, pooling in her pussy. *Fuck!* Priscilla squirmed for a second before giving him a saucy look of her own.

"Well?" she asked, clearly annoyed. This was getting really old, really fast.

He sat up, leaned forward and rested his elbows on his knees. "I sent my best man. The fog was his cover. If you'd been patient, you would have seen him arrive."

Had it been anyone but Zack, Priscilla would have punched him. She didn't know what he'd been up to since he'd left, but if the rumors were to be believed, it had been undercover work for the Archana Council Elders. And that meant if he said he sent his best man, then he did. End of argument.

But she *so* wanted to argue with him.

"Well, it's a damn good thing he showed then. Goodness knows I'm paying you enough for this service."

"About that." Zack stood, blinked and his spilled scotch glass reappeared in his hand.

She watched as he took a sip, her eyes never leaving him. She loved the way the muscles in his throat moved, how she could see the outline of his biceps through his dress shirt. Despite her jilted heart, she couldn't deny that Zack was a hot piece of ass.

Sweet and Spicy Spells

Another snap of his fingers and Priscilla let out a small squeal as her chair quickly moved across the floor to stop at his feet. Her own drink fell to the floor as she clutched the armrests to prevent herself from sliding off the chair. Before she had time to move, much less recover, Zack's hands were on hers to prevent her from quickly escaping from the chair. His body was only inches away and he moved so his face hovered dangerously close to her. Near enough that it would take very little effort to steal a kiss.

Steal a kiss? What the fuck am I thinking!

Priscilla sucked in her bottom lip as she broke the intense eye contact. Instead she enjoyed the close-up view of his neck. A scent she'd forgotten long ago washed over her—a combination of sandalwood, scotch and wizard power. Her body reacted to his proximity, her nipples painfully tightening to rub against her corset. Her skin began to tingle as the heat of his breath rolled over her cheek and neck, sending shivers of awareness through her. *No, no, no!* She wasn't going to let him get to her. She needed to be the one in control.

"We never did discuss payment," he said with his low, rumbling voice.

An image of the two of them naked, rolling around on a king-sized bed, filled Priscilla's mind. She'd lick every inch of his skin, paying particular attention to the sizable cock she'd heard he had between his legs. *By the spells, she was losing it.*

"How about I teach you a few spells. You wizards have such a hard time mastering the simplest earth incantations."

"*Lux lucis ventulus.*"

Priscilla felt a light breeze tickle her legs, blowing the hem of her skirt to expose more of her legs. A shiver ran down her back, but if it was from the wind or Zack, she wasn't sure.

"Impressive. You've been practicing."

Zack smiled. "You'll find I'm better at a lot of things. Years of experience."

21

Christine d'Abo & Renee Field

She knew exactly what he was referring to. Her nipples tingled as his gaze drifted down for a moment before returning to her eyes.

"I very much doubt I'd be surprised by anything you could do in the bedroom. There have been so many men in the past five years. And they were all so *good*." Priscilla sighed as she snuggled back into the seat and hoped she looked more confident than she felt at the moment.

"Let's change the topic, shall we?" he said with a cat-like purr. "Your past conquests aren't important right now."

"But they're important to me. Each and every one of them slamming their cock into me fired me up," she said, and leaned up to lick his cheek. "I've had to fuck a lot of men to get this powerful."

She felt his hands tighten around hers, watched as his pulse beat in his throat.

"I'm changing the topic," he ground out.

She answered instinctively. "You were never good at finishing what you started, were you, Zack?"

"Oh this is very much about finishing what I started. Something I started a few years ago before the council rudely interrupted me."

Priscilla felt her mouth open to speak, but nothing came out. A lot of things had happened five years ago, most of which she'd been able to put behind her. But not Zack. Despite her words, every man she'd been with, she'd compared to him. Which pissed her off to no end when she thought about it. Did she want to go through all this again?

Screw that.

Priscilla leaned forward so her nose brushed his. Her lips were only a hair's distance away. "And what did they so rudely interrupt? I thought you'd tied everything up?"

He didn't back down. Not that she'd expected he would. Instead, Zack smiled and placed a single kiss on the end of her nose.

22

Sweet and Spicy Spells

"Why, winning the Cauldron Cup. What else is there?"

She didn't move. The smile that had been on her lips was still in place, but inside her head Priscilla was screaming *No Fucking Way!* There were a lot of things Zack could do better than she could — pee standing up, for example — but there was no way he could beat her in the Cup.

Priscilla began to laugh. She knew she shouldn't, that it would only serve to piss Zack off more, but she couldn't help it. And she couldn't stop it.

"You want to..." was all she could manage for several minutes.

"I was favored to win before I had to withdraw back then. Besides, I think you've gotten a bit too big for your broomstick, Prissy. I can't wait to bring you down a peg or two."

The dark brown of his eyes was almost swallowed up by the blacks of his pupils. That was a surefire sign that, despite the playfulness in his voice, he was getting pissed off. Priscilla finally managed to stop laughing, and needed a moment to compose herself. Zack didn't move back, keeping his face dangerously close to hers.

When she was finally ready, Priscilla sighed and snuggled down deep into the chair, buying herself another inch of space. "Zack, darling, other wizards have tried. But they just don't have the..." she made a point of looking down at his crotch, "the spells to beat me."

He smiled at her and captured her chin in his hand. The warmth of his skin sunk into hers and she had to fight against the urge to sigh.

"Prissy, my *spells* are more than big enough to handle you."

"That's what they all say. But each and every one of them goes home with a broken wand," she said and winked at him.

She knew better than to taunt a wizard of Zack's power and ability, but she couldn't help it. There was something about him, something that pushed her to the limits of her

23

control and dared her to tease him. For his part, Zack seemed to enjoy their banter, even if she did push him. She doubted anyone dared to take him on and even wizards liked a challenge on occasion.

As long as his wand wasn't getting insulted.

Zack finally sighed, stood up and released Priscilla from his sensual interrogation. Not about to let the opportunity pass, she stood and firmly placed her hands on her hips.

"Who did you send to help my sister through her little bout of performance anxiety?"

"By the *spells*, Prissy, you don't give up, do you? I told you I sent my best man and that's all you need to know. Other than the fact I plan on beating you in the Cup this year. Harry's really can't handle a woman in here. The apparitions have been quite irked."

"I thought they quite enjoyed looking up my skirt. I don't wear any underwear to appease them," she lied. She knew the ghosts preferred it when she wore her thong.

They stood there nose to nose, taunts hovering between them. For a moment, Priscilla wasn't sure how he'd react, but wizard that he was, Zack began to laugh. The vibrations embraced her, wrapping her in warmth and a sense of security. Despite her best efforts, she smiled back.

"I forgot how irrepressible you were," he said and reached out to capture a handful of her black hair.

The contact was gentle, almost caring in its delicate caress as he slid his hand along the strands. Priscilla shivered and tried to ignore any meaning behind it. *Ha! There wouldn't be any meaning*. Not from Zack, who dumped her without so much as a goodbye last time.

"Why do I get the feeling you're trying to avoid my question?" She crossed her arms, erecting a small barrier between them.

"I'm not avoiding it. I don't feel the necessity to answer it."

Sweet and Spicy Spells

"She's my little sister. If our positions were reversed and it was your little brother, you'd want to know every detail."

Zack sighed and turned, shaking his head. Making his way over to the couch, he picked up his book and began to leaf through the pages.

"I doubt Foster would appreciate being referred to as *little*."

"Zack!"

"You're right, I would want to know every detail." He looked up and she could see him gathering the energy in the room. She braced, knowing that he was getting ready to cast a spell, but not knowing what it would be. "But remember, *you* came to me. You begged me to help Kisha with her spell casting impotency and that's what I'm doing. I've given the best wizard next to myself all the information he needs to help her. She'll be ready for her test the night of the Cup and that's all you need to know." He shut the book with a snap. "Case closed."

Priscilla had to shake her head. That was the most he'd said to her since his arrival back. And every word of his little speech pissed her off.

"Let's get something clear. I asked. I never *beg*. And if you want to be a royal ass, go ahead. I can turn you into a toad if you'd like. But know this." She walked over to him, leaned in and whispered in his ear. "If anything bad happens to Kisha, or if she doesn't pass her test, I'm going to personally take it out on your ass."

And to bring her point home, she licked the ridge of his ear. "After I kick it and bring home the Cup for the *sixth* year in a row."

Zack's hand wrapped around her elbow. His grip wasn't firm enough to hurt, but she wasn't going anywhere until he let go.

"Prissy, there is no way in hell I'm going to let you win. By the end of the competition, you'll be begging me to put you out of your misery."

"I told you, I never beg."

"You'll beg me to fuck you senseless."

"I very much doubt that."

"Bet on it?"

By the end of their little exchange, they were both breathing heavily. She was feeling a little high from the familiar potency of his scent. Her pussy was aching and wet. She needed to get the hell out of here so she could clear her head. Maybe find that waiter of hers for a quick fuck. With Zack so close, she found her thoughts constantly drifting back to him. Wanting to strip his clothes off, not with a spell but with her teeth. To suck his cock, lick his balls until he begged her to put him out of his misery and let him fuck her. The only way she was going to get him out of her system was to beat him at his own game. That meant accepting his wager.

"You're on."

Zack chuckled, "That's my girl. If I win the Cup, you have to accept a job as a waitress here at Harry's. Your only job will be to serve me drinks every time I come in. Wearing whatever I want."

The idea of becoming Zack's personal slave had a strangely appealing element to it. Priscilla bit the inside of her cheek before nodding.

"And if I win?"

He shrugged. "Name your price."

The possibilities were endless, but there was something in particular she wanted from him. Something she'd waited for over five years. Priscilla made sure to look him in the eye when she spoke and kept her voice low.

"A date."

Zack frowned. "What?"

Sweet and Spicy Spells

"If I win, you'll owe me a night out. Dinner, dancing, meeting my every whim all night long. You'll smile, laugh, flirt and at the end of the night I get to kick your ass to the curb."

A fire seemed to light in Zack's eyes. She knew he remembered what they'd had planned the night he'd broken things off with her. She would win the Cup and make every second of her prize a living hell for him. Make him realize exactly what he'd walked away from.

"Well?" she asked with as much innocence as she could muster.

"Deal," he said in a clipped tone.

"What's the matter, Zack? You don't want to be seen with me in public?"

"Not at all." He smiled at her once again. "I don't plan on losing."

"Then we don't have any problems."

"Nope."

"Good."

Priscilla wanted to scream. Why the hell did she let him get to her so easily? She was a powerful, sexy witch, with enough going for her to win any man she wanted.

So why was the only thing on her mind winning Zack over?

As suddenly as their conversation started, she felt him begin to pull away from her. Zack stepped back and reclaimed his seat on the couch. She couldn't tell what he was feeling anymore. Shit, she didn't know what *she* was feeling anymore. But she knew something wasn't right. The energy around them began to shimmer once again.

"I hate to chat and run, Prissy, but I need to get back to my place."

"Coward," she said, and rolled her eyes.

His lips pressed together in a thin line. "I've killed men for calling me that."

"Good thing I'm a woman."

He nodded once and let a wicked grin slip onto his face. "Aren't you going to ask what I need to do at home?"

"I really don't give a shit, Zack."

"Oh, I think you should, considering it has to do with your sister."

Priscilla felt every muscle in her back tighten. Whatever it was he was about to tell her, she knew this wasn't going to be good.

"What?" she ground out.

It really pissed her off that he was enjoying this a bit too much.

"I need to get home to check my *top wizard's* report. To find out if *Foster* has thoroughly fucked your sister senseless."

Everything in Priscilla's world stopped. Her body felt like someone had thrown a bucket of cold water on her.

"You sent..."

"My brother. Have a great day, Prissy."

And with a snap of his fingers, Zack disappeared into thin air.

Sweet and Spicy Spells

Chapter Three

ℵ

"I hear you have a little problem," said Foster, startling the witch he assumed to be Kisha—Prissy's little sister.

She whirled around so fast she fell onto the bed, one boot on and the other off. On any other witch, the act would have been comical, on her it was sinfully provocative. She sprawled over the bed with her breasts heaving on the worn cotton bedspread and tempted him like no other. Hell, even his right ball ached for her.

Pink toenails winked at him from the one bare foot he spied. He moved closer, loving how her light hazel eyes glared fury at him.

"You're not real. You're just a fantasy. Okay, my fantasy," she mumbled. "This is just another one of her spells and I am so going to kill her for this one," she said, attempting to scoot farther up the large bed as she gathered some dignity.

Not real. Fantasy. Foster grinned wickedly. She thought of him as a fantasy, and if his cock twitched any more, he'd start to drool. "That's right, Kisha, I'm your fantasy come true." *Boy, when I lie, I lie good.*

She froze and eyed his body from head to toe. A slight blush stole over her features, quickening his heart and fueling the fire that was thickening the blood that went straight to the head of his cock.

"I don't know how she did it, but she's even got your hair right," she said, twisting around so that she now stood at the foot of the bed with one boot on and one off. In her hand was a white, worn sneaker. The other sneaker was half under the bed.

29

Christine d'Abo & Renee Field

He conjured the other sneaker into his hand. "Looking for this?"

She didn't say anything as she tentatively took his offering. He was tempted to pull it back and her with it. Actually, he was really tempted to push her down onto the light blue cotton blanket and strip her bare. *Now that's got merit and purpose all tied up in one neat package.*

He realized she was once again mumbling to herself. Something about damn brown wavy hair, broad shoulders and dangerous green cat eyes. Him. *She's muttering to herself about me…her so-called fantasy lover. Now that's what I call an advantage,* thought Foster.

"Would you like to inspect the package?"

"What?" she stuttered, her cheeks turning as red as those hot lip candies he liked to suck on. "No, you're not real. If I ignore you, she'll see it's not going to work."

Okay, now this wasn't what he wanted. To be ignored when his cock was straining against the tight confines of his jeans. No way. He wanted, make that needed, action.

"Actually, Kisha, I'm real. A living, breathing, throbbing," he arched his eyebrows at her so she'd get his meaning, "wizard. Name's Foster and I've been assigned to you."

"Assigned to me!" she all but screeched. "Do I look like a homework assignment to you?" She marched around the bedroom in tight circles. "Go back. Get out!"

"Make me," he taunted, loving the sway of her small hips as she glared at him. He knew she had no idea how provocative she looked. The blood red shirt detailed every aspect of her well-endowed breasts and he could have sworn he had seen black lace underneath. His fingers twitched to cast the shirt and bra away. For a black moment, he considered resorting to such drastic measures.

But that wouldn't accomplish what he'd been sent here to do. *Then again, what exactly was I sent here to do? And just how can a witch not use her magic?* The mystery of the fiery witch, all

30

Sweet and Spicy Spells

but shooting daggers at him with her light hazel eyes, drew him in like the lure of cotton candy at a fair. Both went hand in hand and both were sweet and melted in his mouth.

First it was hot lips, then it was cotton candy, boy do I ever need to get laid, thought Foster. He forced the imagery of the tantalizing sweets out of his mind, which was so far in the gutter he could barely breathe. *I want her. I want that witch panting with need*, he thought, amazed at how much the tiny woman invigorated him within only five minutes of meeting her.

"Make me leave. If you can," he mocked, cocking one of his eyebrows up as he sexily grinned at her. Foster realized then that he hadn't had so much fun in years.

"I can if I want to," she chimed.

But her eyes were the dead giveaway. Fear. Deep-rooted fear stared back at him. Why? What made her so afraid of the magic that ran inherent in her cells that she couldn't, or wouldn't, do it?

Foster sauntered over to the bed and flopped down on it, bracing his arms behind his head so he could watch the utterly astonished look on her face.

"Get off my bed, you lug," she said, moving an inch closer to the bed. He just knew she wanted to stamp that tiny foot of hers, but she checked that urge quickly when she noticed he was watching and waiting for a reaction. "You're doing this on purpose just to provoke me."

"Yup, I am. Still thinking I'm your fantasy lover because, sweetlips, I'm so liking that notion," teased Foster as he patted the spot next to him on the small bed.

"Are you always like this?"

The question momentarily caught him off guard. "Like what?"

"Like an asshole, you idiot," she said, the fire once again alive and sparkling in her hazel eyes.

Christine d'Abo & Renee Field

"You ain't even seen my ass, sweetlips, but if you'd like to take a look, go for it. *Aufero vestitus*!"

In a flash, Foster was buck-naked, standing in the middle of the bedroom flashing his backside at her. Drastic measures. But a wizard's gotta do what a wizard's gotta do. Especially if said wizard has a raging hard-on that is cutting circulation off to his legs because of his bloody jeans. He was tired of talking and his cock certainly wanted some affection from those tiny, delicate hands of hers. But laughter was the last thing he was expecting. *If she thinks my ass is funny, quid pro quo*, he thought, a second before he heard her sputter and dive under the blankets on the bed.

"I can't believe you did that. You have five seconds to give me back my clothes," she demanded, clutching the cotton blanket all the way up to her neck.

"You know, I could blink away all those blankets?" he teased, turning to provide her with a full frontal view of the wizard he was. He could have sworn her eyes widened with interest a moment before she clamped them shut.

"Don't be a prude, take a look."

"Fuck you," she said, clenching her eyes tighter.

He moved quickly onto the bed and braced his weight over her as she lay perfectly still. "Actually, sweetlips, that's exactly what I intend to do to you. A good long fuck, and by the by, have you got any chocolate? I'm famished for something sweet. Ahh, don't bother, I've got the feeling that once I taste you—"

"Get off me. Now!" she demanded, still not opening her eyes.

"Open your eyes, sweetlips."

She attempted to knee him through the blankets. Foster was having none of that. He squatted so that she was captured between his thighs while he kept most of his weight off her. He didn't want to squish the tiny witch.

32

Sweet and Spicy Spells

"Stop calling me that," she squeaked, still clutching the blanket for her life.

"What?"

"Sweetlips."

Her eyes flickered open for a fraction of a second before she clenched them closed again. Foster leaned over her, a breath away from those lips of hers that he desperately wanted to taste. He felt her stiffen, as if she knew what he intended. He delicately swirled his tongue over her still-clenched lips and tasted the ambrosia of her—chocolate chip cookies—as he inhaled her unique womanly scent that reminded him of vanilla.

Now that's not fair. Her lips taste like cookies. He couldn't help himself, never could when it came to snacks. He leaned even more over her and forced his tongue between her lips. It only took a second before he felt her relax, before her mouth opened on its own accord, before her tongue snaked out to greet him. Heaven! He'd gone straight to heaven and he had a sneaking suspicion that she was going to be one hell of a ride.

"This isn't going to work," she mumbled against his lips.

"Work? Sweetlips, trust me on this one, all my parts work," he replied, his chest heaving as he moved off her lips and lowered the blanket. Her ivory-colored neck dotted with light brown freckles begged to be licked and nipped.

"Sex won't make it happen," she declared sadly.

The urge to tell the witch to shut up slammed hot into him.

"I've had sex, lots of it, and nothing. Not a zap, not an itch, nothing."

He stilled. The idea of her having sex with other men didn't appeal one bit to the wizard he was. And why that idea rankled him mystified him. Later, once he'd eased the ache in his balls, he'd think more about that. For now, actions spoke louder than words.

"Sweetlips, I'm your cure."

33

Christine d'Abo & Renee Field

She laughed again, the sound startlingly sexy. But nothing Foster said was remotely funny.

"Cure? You're the man my sister sent to help me. Give me a break," she said, attempting to buck him off her.

Now that movement Foster liked. A lot. But what he also wanted was her body on fire just like his was.

"Sorry, honey, I ain't a man. I'm your noble wizard at your disposable. And I do intend to cure you." Foster lowered his lips so he could kiss that neck of hers that drew his eyes.

"Fine, get it over with," she said, with about as much enthusiasm as someone clipping their nails.

Now it was Foster's turn to laugh. *Get it over with.* Just what the fuck did she think he was? Then again, he didn't really have a plan, so maybe this was the "in" he was looking for.

He zapped away the blanket that was covering that luscious body he keenly wanted to feel and savor, all before she could take her next breath. She stilled again but wisely remained silent. This time it was he who wanted to close his eyes as those appraising green eyes of hers, speckled with hues of brown, stared at him with such intent.

"Like I said, get it over with," she muttered again, trying for a bored tone in her voice, but her puckered nipples were a giveaway.

She was enjoying their battle of wills as much as his body was enjoying the satiny feel of her pale skin, which was in direct contrast to his tanned body. *They do say opposites attract.* He gulped as his eyes traveled the length of her. Two beautiful firm round globes swayed slightly as she moved beneath him and then he looked, he couldn't help it. He had to see if she was a real redhead. *Yup, like I thought, she's the real deal.* Slightly darker than the hair on her head, the red curls peeked at him, calling his name, and he wasn't about to disappoint.

Sweet and Spicy Spells

He slid down the length of her body, bypassing those two delicious breasts of hers that screamed a slight protest, but it was time he took matters into his own hands.

"What are you doing?" she said, lifting her body slightly up off the bed so she could watch him.

"Cotton candy."

"What?" she asked, wrinkling her tiny nose that was dusted with light brown freckles.

He planned to kiss each and every one of those freckles at another time. He moved even lower and maneuvered his body between her legs, making her yield. Still partially propped up, she warily watched him. It pleased him to note she did move her legs, providing him with the best view in the house — her already-glistening pussy.

Without waiting another second, he lowered his head and inhaled her unique scent. Her musky sex, combined with vanilla, washed into his senses and went straight to his throbbing cock.

"Like what you see?" she asked.

Her response surprised him. *Ahh, there is a wild side to her,* he thought with relish. "Actually I love what I see a lot, but I'm going to really enjoy licking your cream."

He watched as her chest rose, and her pupils dilated with sexual understanding. *She likes it when I talk dirty. Now that's got its appeal, big time.*

"Trust me, it won't matter."

"Sweetlips, it all matters. Every inch of you matters," he said, diving in. *Fuck, she does taste like cotton candy.* That was his first thought as his tongue circled her already swollen nether lips. He lapped up the white cream along her cunt and then plunged his tongue into her tight opening, licking her candied juices. *I'm going to have a sugar rush* was his second thought, and his third was, *What a way to die.*

She mewed in delight, her sounds turning him on even more. He felt her fingers glide through and then grasp the hair on his head as she repositioned his mouth to just where she wanted it the most. Not yet, he thought, moving his tongue to a slower tempo as he swirled it back and forth over her glistening lips.

"Right there," she gasped, arching her body up off the bed.

"Where?" he whispered the words into her pussy, blowing cool air over her swollen clit. He watched as it pebbled even more.

"You know where," she said, still gasping but slightly annoyed, he noted.

"Show me, sweetlips. Show me what you want me to suck."

He felt her body stiffen. Maybe she wasn't ready, he thought. No, she had to. He somehow knew this was exactly the right prescription for her. She had to overcome her sexual limitations. She had to step out of her comfort zone.

He moved farther off the bed, so that his legs were now on the wooden floor. He yanked her naked body down with him and then flipped her legs over his shoulders, exposing her wet pussy to the cool bedroom air and to his penetrating eyes. The sight of her like that was sexy as sin. He grasped his cock with one hand for a hard stroke, trying to ease the ache.

He blew on her nub again. "Show me. You can do it, sweetlips."

She thrashed her head from side to side on the bed. "I can't…I can't." The words were almost an incoherent mumble. She was so on the edge he could see her tight opening clenching in sweet anticipation of his hard cock sliding into her.

He tapped on her nub with one hand. She squirmed even more with need. "Show me," he demanded, giving in to the urge to lick her cotton-candied juices one more time. He lapped her with his tongue, one long hard lick from the crack of her ass to her cunt. She mewed as need took over.

Sweet and Spicy Spells

"Show me," he said, gently tapping again on her pebbled tight nub.

She arched up off the bed so fast, it surprised him. "There…please," she said, opening her nether lips with her own hand so that her prized clit, swollen with need, gleamed at him.

"Say it."

"Wha—"

"Tell me what you want me to suck. Say it, Kisha," said Foster, thinking he really could be a bastard sometimes.

He thought for a moment she rolled her eyes. "Fine, suck my clit. There, are you—"

He stopped her in mid-sentence as his teeth gently nipped at her nub. She leaned back on her arms, still watching him work her pussy. Her head was thrown back as the sensation of her climax started to ride all her nerve endings.

"That's it, my witch, come for me," he said, nudging his nose into her wet juices, lapping her pussy greedily. He plunged first one finger into her wet cunt and then slid it out to play with the crack of her ass. She slightly arched off the bed, almost begging for his finger, his attentions. He plunged two fingers into her pussy and moved his hand, rotating his fingers so he could hit her ultra-sensitive spot. Her umph of surprise told him he had it. It also told him no other man had ever found it. His wizardly ego inflated with the idea of being the first to make her come hard simply with his tongue and finger.

"That's it, sweetlips, come for me," he said, pulling her tight nub into his mouth. He felt her spread her legs more, yield more to his demands and then, whammooo—he was sailing through the air in the bedroom. Foster cracked his head hard on the wall.

"What the fuck just happened?" Foster was pissed to the core that he'd missed making Kisha come.

37

Christine d'Abo & Renee Field

Kisha's look of total surprise, combined with that unfulfilled sexual look, was almost amusing.

"I'm so sorry," she mumbled, scurrying to a sitting position on the bed.

"You did that?"

"I think. I was thinking…this was going to be an amazing climax, or maybe I thought explosion, but somehow that happened."

Normally, Foster would have been amused by a declaration like this. Now, however, he wasn't. He rubbed his head with his hand. Well, who said it was going to be easy? He walked back to the bed. "I'm thinking you might have to kiss it to make it better."

She moved closer to the edge of the bed. "Bend down. I can't reach your head."

"Sweetlips, you most certainly can," he said, taking his still raging cock in his hand so she'd get his meaning. He watched as her pink tongue darted out to wet her lips.

She smiled. "I do believe it's the least I can do, but don't say I didn't warn you."

"Well, warn all the way, because I plan to get a bellyache of cotton candy before noon and I like it that way," he said, grinning.

"What's with you and candy?" she asked, a moment before her warm lips took the head of his cock into the recesses of her mouth.

He went dizzy with need and fought not to buck his hips forward, the urge to ram his rod down her throat riding him fast. She sucked hard, taking more of his girth in her mouth, and then her small hands cupped his balls. He could have sworn he saw stars. It took a lot of concentration to not climax. Her touch was so gentle, so loving and so damned skillful. First she rolled his right ball in her hand and then toyed with his sac while moving a hand to play with the crack of his ass. She wasn't shy and he liked that.

Sweet and Spicy Spells

However, he had been assigned to teach her to use her magic and as much as it would probably kill him he was going to have to remove his cock from her warm, wet mouth and make her come.

Slowly he moved back, forcing his raging hard-on out of her inviting mouth. Her lips were swollen. He leaned over and kissed her while his hands went to her breasts. He tweaked both nipples hard, enjoying her gasp.

"You do understand that I'm going to have to make you come?"

"Is that supposed to be a threat?"

"We're going to do it my way." A moment later, Foster zapped Kisha into position.

"I can't believe you're serious," she said, giving in to a slightly terrified giggle as she yanked on the black rope that anchored both her arms to the two bedposts.

"You know you could zap yourself out of them," he replied smoothly, allowing her to believe she could get control of the current situation she'd found herself in.

"If I wanted to," she said, giving a yank to the black rope that anchored both her arms to the two bedposts.

"That's good," he said, a moment before he zapped a blindfold over her eyes. "Don't panic. I need you to relax, enjoy and let the magic fuel your body and mind. Trust me."

"Trust you…I don't even know you and I can't believe I'm even doing this. I am going to kill my sister," she said, attempting to move her legs, which were spread-eagled and tied to the bottom bedposts.

"I can certainly tell you that I plan to personally thank your sister. This is the best assignment I've ever had. Like I said earlier, losing does have merit. Now where was I before I got rudely thrown across the room? Ahh, here I was," he said, sliding in between her legs. Her scent was stronger, as was her need, he thought, watching as her sweet juices coated the

39

Christine d'Abo & Renee Field

insides of her thighs. He licked first one thigh and then the other.

He grasped her ass and moved her bottom slightly off the bed, providing him with better leverage to suck her dry. Within minutes she was teetering on the brink of a climax. Foster felt his body stiffen and he almost chuckled, realizing he was waiting for another whammo. When none came, he moved his tongue up and nipped her nub, while one hand moved to tweak a puckered nipple. She arched her body, almost trembling with the need for release. His tongue lapped more of her candied juices as they started to drip out of her wet pussy. The taste was even sweeter than before.

He heard her cry out his name, then a bright flash filled the small bedroom and he was once again sailing fast toward the wall. This time he was ready. He willed himself to stop just before impact. A second later, when he looked around the room, he cursed loudly. Shit, she was gone. He could just imagine what had been racing through her mind, her body on the verge of climaxing, her come almost pouring into his mouth. He shook his head. For all he knew, she had willed herself to Iceland. The idea of something cold actually sounded good to his raging hard-on, which throbbed tightly for release.

For a moment, Foster was tempted to take matters into his own hands, but then thought better of it. He had a witch to track and he planned on using every wizard spell he had learned to get Kisha to come hard while screaming his name again and again. Then, and only then, would he get the release he desperately needed.

Sweet and Spicy Spells

Chapter Four

ဆ

Zack was standing at the bar in his condo, mixing a Blue Lagoon. He'd already poured himself three fingers of his best scotch and was sipping it, getting ready for the blast that was sure to come. He knew it was only a matter of time before Prissy would show up. And he'd be lucky to survive the first five minutes of that conversation. His only chance would be to keep her occupied long enough to get her drunk. Even *she* couldn't cast while shit-faced.

The pang of regret he'd felt at seeing her come up the stairs at Harry's had quickly been replaced with raging lust. He was still trying to remember all the reasons he'd walked away from her. None of them seemed overly convincing any longer. Priscilla had obviously been hurt by what he'd done to her, but he couldn't regret the decision he'd made back then.

The wind picked up and blasted his curtains from the half-open window. That was all the warning he got that Priscilla was on her way. In a poof of red smoke, she appeared in the middle of his living room floor. Immediately, she turned to face him and he saw the rage in her eyes. She was panting hard, thrusting the tops of her breasts so high they threatened to spill from her corset. Fuck, she was one hot witch.

"You sent Foster!"

"I told you I'd send the best and I did."

"*Foster!*"

Zack sighed and dropped a cherry into her drink. He knew she wouldn't cross the floor and come to him, no matter how pissed off she was. It was time to prove he was really as good as he told the council. Zack sauntered over, ignoring the stinging sensations on the bottoms of his feet as he walked. He

41

Christine d'Abo & Renee Field

wasn't about to give her the satisfaction of knowing her pain spell was working.

"You didn't finish your drink," he said and smiled as he handed her the glass.

"Fuck you, Zack." Priscilla crossed her arms across her chest. "If you think for one moment that I'm going to let Foster ruin Kisha's life, then you're as stupid as you look."

Every muscle in his body stiffened. Zack was used to people attacking him, even women as beautiful as Prissy. But when it came to his family, he didn't take any shit. In the blink of an eye, he sent the drink back to the bar so he was free of any impediments. He was about to grab her arms but shoved his hands in his pockets instead. That wasn't anyway to win her over. *Why the hell do I care if I win her over?* He forced a breath and hoped it would be enough to keep his temper in check.

"And why do you think Foster would do anything to Kisha other than what *you* asked him to do? Hmm? He doesn't have a cruel bone in his body."

"Bullshit. He's a Kane and you're all the same."

Zack didn't even realize he'd grabbed her until they landed with a thud against the wall. They were both panting, her breasts rubbing against his chest. He couldn't take his eyes off hers and he could see her inner fire matched his. She'd be more than a match for him both in and out of bed. His cock agreed, twitching at the hint of arousal coming from her. He hadn't wanted to fuck a woman this much in years.

"And what the hell is that supposed to mean?" he ground out.

To her credit, Priscilla didn't look surprised. She kept her cool and despite her passion simmering just below the surface, she kept her emotions in check. Which was better than he was doing.

"It means he'll take advantage of her, fuck her and walk away without really helping her. Kisha isn't as sure of herself

42

Sweet and Spicy Spells

as she should be. The last thing she needs is a head trip from your brother."

Zack shifted his weight so he was better able to pin Priscilla's wrists to the wall. Every inch of her body was now pressed against his and damn it if his body didn't notice. Despite his annoyance, his cock sprang to life and began to press against her stomach. There wasn't any hiding his arousal from her and Zack wanted to groan when she began to grin.

"I see some things never change."

"And what's that, Prissy?"

"That I'm still the best cock-tease out there."

He immediately released her hands, spun around and stalked back to the bar. Zack downed the entire contents of his scotch glass in one gulp before refilling it and taking another deep drink. How the hell had he lost control of the situation so quickly? No one did this to him, especially not a woman.

Not that Priscilla *was* a typical woman.

"You really enjoy pushing people's buttons, don't you, Prissy?"

"About as much as you enjoy pushing mine."

He heard her snap her fingers and the Blue Lagoon was suddenly back in her hands. When Zack faced her again, he was amazed at how much sex appeal radiated from her. She'd always been sexy, but now she was sinfully tempting. Every wizard's wet dream. Thank the spells they'd never mind linked years ago. He really didn't need her hearing his thoughts right now.

Priscilla sipped her drink, not once taking her eyes from him. Her constant scrutiny made his cock pulse as the blood began to pound through his body. No, he couldn't let her get the better of him.

"I want you to call Foster off. Find another wizard to help Kisha."

Christine d'Abo & Renee Field

With a sly smile of his own, Zack whispered a quick spell under his breath. When she didn't flinch, he knew it had landed successfully. This would prove very entertaining.

"And why would I do that?"

She tightened her grip on her glass. "I've already given you my reasons. I don't trust you or your brother. Please, Zack."

He almost felt guilty about not backing down. *Almost.* But as Priscilla brought the glass to her mouth, ready to sip her drink, that guilt quickly faded. When the glass reached her lips and she took a taste, Priscilla's boots poofed away.

"What the hell?"

"All Kisha needs is someone who can break down her insecurities and give her a confidence boost. She has the potential to be a very powerful witch."

Priscilla was busy looking at her feet. "Where are my boots? Those were expensive."

"You were marking my floor," he took a sip of his scotch and sat down in his leather armchair. He wanted to be comfortable for the impending show.

Priscilla snapped her fingers and her boots reappeared. "I've tried to help build her confidence. I've taken her on assignments for the council. We even did a few midnight conjuring sessions. But it didn't seem to help."

Another sip of her drink and her corset poofed away. The sudden appearance of her full breasts made his mouth water. He wanted to suck those perky nipples until she screamed his name.

"Zack! What the fuck are you *doing*?"

He didn't mean to laugh, but he couldn't help it. "That's all you, baby."

Priscilla actually growled at him as she snapped her fingers to get her corset back. Another quick snap and Zack found himself without his shirt. He knew she'd expect him to

44

Sweet and Spicy Spells

play along with her counterattack and get it back, but he had other plans. The already warm air of his condo had heated up more with Priscilla's arrival. He finished the contents of his glass and enjoyed the mellow buzz the alcohol gave him.

"I don't think you realize how intimidating you can be, Prissy. You've probably scared poor Kisha half to death with all of your *help*."

Zack's cock twitched as Priscilla's gaze traveled across his naked chest. He'd spent just as much time in the gym as he had out in the field. He couldn't afford to show any weakness in his line of work, either mentally or physically. Some of his spells took every ounce of strength from him. However, it also had the added bonus of making him particularly attractive to women. And at the moment, there was one witch whom he wanted to distract, and he was more than happy to use his body to do it.

"I'm...not intimidating. I'm practically a pussycat," she said as her gaze flicked between his chest and his eyes.

Her grip flexed around the glass, but she didn't take another sip. Knowing she needed a bit more incentive, Zack sat forward and rested his arms on his knees. He even flexed his biceps a little and wanted to laugh as her eyes followed the movement.

"The only time you're a pussycat is when you transform into one. Let's face it, darling, you're more of a panther on the prowl than a lap cat."

His shift in position helped. Priscilla brought the glass to her lips and took not one but two gulps of the blue liquid, draining it. Zack felt his mouth go dry as she now stood before him, dressed only in a black lace thong.

Five years ago, when they were dating, he'd been seriously attracted to Priscilla, but it hadn't gone beyond some heavy petting. She'd been gentler back then. Now he cursed the fact that his job had taken him away from what could have been. With a body like that, he'd never get out of bed.

Christine d'Abo & Renee Field

Priscilla tossed the now empty glass aside and stood with her hands on her hips. Her breasts swayed with the movement and Zack couldn't take his eyes off them. He just about came in his pants.

"Potent drink. You should get a job at Harry's."

Zack had a sneaking suspicion he'd just lost round one. He was okay with defeat if it meant he got to stare at such a beautiful, mostly naked woman. Priscilla was in as good a shape as he was. Her extra-long legs were firm and begged for him to run his hands along them. He knew if she turned around her ass would be perfect. Her stomach was flat and her breasts were big enough to fill his hands. It was enough to give a man a heart attack.

Or, at the very least, a stiff cock.

Not trusting his voice, Zack stood and sauntered over to her. As he walked, pieces of his clothing began to disappear one by one. First his socks and shoes, then his belt and even his underwear, until he was left with only his pants.

Stopping a few inches away from her, Zack could feel Priscilla's body heat rolling off her. The light scent of her vanilla perfume was a distracting contradiction from her personality. Prissy was anything but sweet. She was hot and spicy, just the way he liked it.

"Foster is going to do *whatever* it takes to help Kisha. You know that as well as I. The real question is, are you ready to pay for services rendered?" Zack kept his voice low, smooth, and hoped it would lull her inner beast enough to let him get closer.

"Payment?"

He watched as her eyelids closed a fraction and her body relaxed as he spoke. He was thankful for his pants right then, as he was sure his cock would take over. In no time, he'd be pounding into her wet cunt for no other reason than the sexy look she was giving him right now.

46

Sweet and Spicy Spells

Zack leaned in close to her ear and whispered, "Payment."

"The check…is in…the mail."

Priscilla was panting, each breath pushing her breasts harder against his chest. He felt her body shiver when he placed a kiss in the hollow of her neck where it met her shoulder. Still, he held back, knowing it would be too easy to lose control with her.

"I don't think you're ready to take me on, Prissy. Despite what you'd like people to think, you're a big softy."

"Taking you on isn't much of a challenge," she said with a smirk. Priscilla ran her tongue over her bottom lip and leaned in so she was only an inch away. "But I don't think you're ready for *me*."

Whatever he was about to say would have to come later, because in the next heartbeat Priscilla was kissing him. Her soft lips pulled him close and her tongue began to wickedly explore his mouth. She tasted sinfully spicy, which made his head buzz, and he wanted to eat her whole. She was sexier than he remembered, his body on fire for her.

Her arms were around his neck, pulling him close as she tasted him. He moved his hands down her arms and over her body, stopping to linger on her breasts, stomach and ass. *Spells*, she was perfect. Every inch of her skin was soft and inviting and she melted against his every touch. She responded to him like no other woman ever had. Moaning and writhing against him. *Hot and spicy.*

"You taste so fucking good," he groaned as he grabbed her hips and thrust against her pelvis.

"Shut up and fuck me," she said and pulled him close for another kiss.

Zack lost the ability to think clearly. Instead of casting a spell, he found himself fumbling with the thin material of her thong, pulling it against her cunt. Gently he tugged it over and over, using the material to rub her swollen clit until he felt her gasp against his lips.

"So hot," he whispered against her temple. "I'm going to suck your nipples until you scream."

"Fuck, Zack!"

When she pushed his head toward her breast, Zack didn't hesitate. He slid his knee between her legs to keep her from slipping to the floor as he devoured her breast. Over and over, he flicked his tongue over the swollen and pebbled nipple. Priscilla flexed her fingers in his hair, moaning her encouragement. When he felt her body begin to shake, he moved to her other breast to begin his sensual torture over again.

"If you…stop, I'll…turn you into a toad."

He stood up and she groaned. Her eyes were shut tight and her breathing was coming out in shuttering gasps. Without missing a beat, he continued to roll her nipple between his fingers.

"But if I don't stop, I won't be able to do this."

His fingers pushed past the thin barrier of her thong and brushed the outer lips of her pussy. Priscilla sucked in a breath, but her body instantly stilled. Again Zack brushed the swollen lips, careful to avoid touching her clit. The last thing he wanted was her coming too quickly.

The scent of her arousal was everywhere. The dampness from her pussy trickled down her leg and covered his fingers. Withdrawing his hand, he waited for her to open her eyes before licking her juices off his fingers.

"So fucking hot," he whispered.

Priscilla's eyes widened and for a second, Zack saw her long-gone innocence. He had to wonder if anyone had willingly given themselves to her before. He knew she was used to taking what she wanted rather than letting it come to her. He doubted she would have let anyone get that close.

Sweet and Spicy Spells

"I'm going to eat you now, Prissy. I'm going to lick your cunt over and over until you come all over my face. Then I'm going to fuck you 'til you come again."

Her eyes widened for a fraction of a second before she let them flutter close. That was all the permission he needed. Zack dropped to his knees in front of her. Down there, all he could smell was her unique scent, a mix of vanilla and spice. It poured over him in waves when he pulled her thong aside to see her perfectly shaven pussy. There was no hiding her swollen clit from his hot gaze—and what a sight it was.

Sticking his finger in his mouth to wet it, he traced a line from the top of her clit down over the nub. She cried out when his nail lightly scraped over the sensitive spot, but it didn't stop him. Zack slid his finger into her cunt and curled it so he could reach her G-spot. Her fingers were instantly in his hair, pulling his face into her.

"Who am I to keep a lady waiting?" he muttered a fraction of an inch from her clit.

With unerring precision, he licked up her clit. Priscilla's legs began to tremble against his arms. Zack licked again, savoring every drop of the cream he collected on his tongue. It tasted better than food, or scotch, and it was wholly Priscilla. It made his head spin, the heady aroma making him drunk. Needing to feel her release, taste just how sweet she could be, he began to pump his finger in and out of her pussy. Her muscles clenched at him with every stroke, as if she were trying to stop him from retreating. A second finger only added to her pleasure and the amount of her juices that flowed down his arm.

Zack increased the pressure of his tongue, flicking it madly over her clit. Her fingers squeezed his hair painfully, but he didn't give a shit. When he sucked her swollen nub into his mouth, Priscilla cried out. Her juices flowed down his hand, arm and face as she came.

"Fuck!" she cried as her legs gave out. Somewhere behind him a lamp went flying, smashing against the wall. He released her pussy and let her collapse into his arms.

Her heart was pounding hard and loud in her chest, blended with her steady panting. He damn well better be living up to her expectations, because she'd more than surpassed his.

"So very hot," he murmured and placed a kiss on her temple.

"You're not getting off that easily," she said and pulled back to look at him.

For a moment, he thought she was going to kiss him. Instead she leaned in and licked a drop of her come from his face. "I think it's my turn."

Before he realized what she was doing, Zack was pushed onto his back. His damn pants were still on and pulled tightly across his cock.

"I believe you are a bit overdressed, Mr. Kane."

"Why don't you do something to assist me, Ms. Morgan?"

"Oh, I plan on it. Don't you worry."

Priscilla rolled off him so she could kneel beside his thigh. Her breasts swung seductively just out of reach and Zack wanted to suckle them again. He would have, but in that instant she cast a spell and the zipper on his pants began to roll down on its own. Zack would have laughed that she wasn't doing it herself, except for the fact her hands were busy pulling at her own nipples.

"Do you like it when I play with myself?" she asked in a breathy whisper.

"You're torturing me, Prissy."

"Do you?"

"What do you think?"

He grabbed her hand and shoved it down the opening of his pants to rest on his hot shaft. Her eyes widened again, but

Sweet and Spicy Spells

this time only for a second. Her surprise was quickly replaced by a seductive smile.

"You brought all that for me, Zack? I'm flattered." She curled her fingers around his cock and squeezed.

Thankfully, she didn't draw her teasing out too long. He lifted his hips to help her when she finally pulled his pants down over his hips. Now free, his cock sprang proudly straight up into the air. It was his turn to smile when Priscilla gasped.

"What's the matter, Prissy? Don't think you can handle me?"

It didn't take her long to recover from her surprise. Zack's eyes were locked on her, watching her body as she leaned forward and placed her nose against the tip of his head. He felt her take a deep breath, causing his cock to twitch.

"I want to watch you suck me," he whispered, not caring how desperate he sounded.

"I wonder how you'll taste?"

Zack watched as her tongue darted out to trace a path around the tip of his cock-head.

"Yum, good enough to eat."

Without another word, she dipped her face down and licked from his balls up his shaft to his swollen purple tip, before impaling her mouth on his cock. Zack dug his nails into the floor and tried to hold on as Priscilla's head bobbed up and down on him, sucking and swallowing him. Her hair fell down over her shoulders to tickle the sensitive skin around his groin. It was almost too much for him.

He felt his balls tighten, drawing up close to his body as her fingers worked their magic. *Spells*, it wouldn't be long at all. But despite his thrusting, Priscilla didn't increase her pace.

"You are so fucking unbelievable. I want you to ride me," he ground out.

"Yes."

51

Christine d'Abo & Renee Field

In the next heartbeat, she'd swung her leg over his body and was positioning him at the entrance of her pussy. Slowly, she lowered her weight onto him, inch by blessed inch. Her muscles gripped him as she began to rock her weight up and down on him. Zack clutched her hips and began to thrust hard and fast into her.

"Shit," she moaned.

He could feel her body begin to vibrate and knew she was close to a second orgasm. In a single motion, he captured her breast in his hand and leaned forward to suck on her sensitive nipples. All at once her pussy began to clench around him and she cried out. Frantically, she thrashed on top of his body, pounding out every last wave of pleasure from him.

With what little strength he had left, Zack rolled Priscilla onto her back and covered her body with his. He unleashed everything he had, thrusting madly into her. Crying out, his body tightened until he couldn't breathe. He felt his cum shoot out of him in powerful spurts, filling her completely. They both collapsed into a sweaty, panting heap in the middle of the room.

"Holy shit," she whispered against his neck.

"I agree."

A sudden wave of gentleness came over him and he placed a tender kiss on her neck. Somehow it felt right, something he should have done before he'd walked out on her. If things had only been different five years ago...

But there was no use wondering about what could have been. He had to focus on the future. If he was going to get through to her and convince her he wasn't the bastard she thought, he had a hell of a lot of work ahead of him. And there was no time like the present to start.

Zack looked down at her and gave her a lop-sided grin. "I see we find ourselves in an interesting position."

She raised an eyebrow. "Oh?"

"I believe I'm on top."

Sweet and Spicy Spells

"So?"

"Winners always come out on top."

Chapter Five

Mortified would not begin to describe how Kisha felt. Twice in less than half an hour she'd messed up big time. Really big time. She knew Foster was probably laughing that gorgeous ass of his off at her right that very moment. She groaned loudly, finally forced to take in her surroundings. Shelves of books kept her hidden for the moment. She was at least thankful she'd inadvertently zapped herself somewhere indoors. And miracle of all miracles, no other person was around. She'd take that as a step in the right direction today. After all, what else could go wrong? Twice. Twice she'd been on the verge of having the best orgasm, wait, make that the only orgasm she'd ever had with a man and twice she'd messed up. Could life get any crueler? Wait, it could, she thought, realizing she was still naked.

"I take it you like to read books."

Kisha closed her eyes even as her cheeks blossomed bright pink. She whirled around and crossed her arms over her heaving breasts.

"It took me a moment to trace you, but I decided to follow that sweet scent of yours, which is better than the smell of these dusty relics."

Kisha knew exactly what he meant. Most of the books were lined with at least half an inch of dust. She fought not to sneeze as the dust teased her nose.

"Okay, that's cute. You've found me, so do me a favor and zap us out of here and while you're at it, I'd like my clothes back."

"Now, now, now...that would take all the fun out of this situation. Plus, I was sent to teach you how to use your

Sweet and Spicy Spells

powerful magic and that's exactly what I plan to do. Funny that we should end up here," said Foster, looking at the many books lining the majestic bookshelves.

His words, "powerful magic", stole into her thoughts. It was the first time anyone in her life, besides her great-aunt, thought of her as a powerful witch. She shook her head. The reality of her current situation wasn't lost on her. "It's just a library," she replied wearily, hoping he'd stop stirring up dust from the books with his fingers. Fingers she was trying hard not to notice. Still though the wicked memory of where his fingers had been caused her body to tingle in her most intimate places.

"Actually, it's not just a library. We're in the Archana Council library."

Kisha couldn't help but shiver with his declaration even as her eyes scanned the backs of the ancient-looking books. One particularly large volume, which was cleared of dust, leapt out at her. *Black Magic versus White Magic: The Pros and Cons in Today's Modern World.*

She forced her eyes to move beyond the lure of the book, hating how the words *black magic* thrummed into her subconscious like a slithering snake. *I can't believe I zapped myself here. I can't believe just how stupid I really am. I don't deserve to be called a witch.*

Foster moved two feet closer to her. She felt his body heat and smelled the masculine fresh pine scent of him even though they weren't touching. "Something grab your fancy, sweetlips?"

She shook her head negatively and rubbed her hands up and down her chilled arms. Kisha wasn't sure if she was cold from the temperature or the sheer terror of the situation she currently found herself in.

"It's okay. No one is here and no one can see us," he said, grinning like the sneaky devil-wizard he was, she thought.

Christine d'Abo & Renee Field

"Thank you," she replied. "But seriously, can we finish what we started back in my bedroom?" Kisha hated how pleading her voice sounded even to her own ears.

Foster took another step toward her. He was a breath away and it took a lot of willpower for Kisha to stand her ground. She couldn't believe how much he looked like her fantasy lover. His dark brown hair fell loose to his shoulders and his emerald-green eyes quite literally took her breath away. But it was his ass that caused her to clench and unclench her hands, which were itching to squeeze those tight buns of his.

For a moment she thought it wasn't fair that he resembled her fantasy lover so much, but then she fondly thought of the feel of his tongue and his fingers as they worked her body. She shivered again with need. His pine scent combined with that masculine pheromone he must somehow be emitting went straight to her still-pulsing cunt. She wished she could cross her legs or rub her body up and down the length of him to ease the ache within her. When he tweaked a stray hair behind her ear, she realized she hadn't heard a word he had said.

"What?" she asked, feeling slightly foolish.

A smug grin spread across his face. "I see you were daydreaming again about me," he said teasingly. "To clarify, you are going to have to earn your way out of here."

"Earn my way out of here? What are you talking about?"

"You need first to conjure up the clothing I deem you will wear and you need to get it right. Then, and only then, will we zap together to another much more comfortable place."

"Clothing you deem I should wear? I'm not liking this joke anymore," she said, slightly alarmed with the idea. With how her spells were working lately, she had a sinking feeling she'd end up wearing some sort of sick, fuzzy, pink bunny costume equipped with a real tail. *Now how childish would that be? A lot*, she thought, squeamish with the idea of his little test.

56

Sweet and Spicy Spells

"No joke. Matching pink bra and thong," he said, grinning ear-to-ear.

"Yeah right," she hissed at him.

Kisha watched Foster cross his arms over his muscular chest.

"It's up to you, Kisha. Either you conjure up the clothing I say or you stay naked. Frankly, I'm all for you staying naked, but then again, I'm not saying how long my shield will work."

"You wouldn't?" she squeaked.

"I would. You have five minutes to conjure up items one and two."

Kisha felt her eyebrows furrow together. Panic seized her chest.

"Take a breath, you can do it, just relax."

"Relax, you can—"

"Four minutes and counting."

Kisha shut her mouth. She closed her eyes and concentrated hard. *I can do this. I can do this,* she chanted in her head, and then she felt it. *Vestitus!* The word flew out of her mouth and the feel of smooth satin covered her heaving chest. She grinned. "I did it."

"Sadly, you did," he replied, still grinning. "Now conjure up a low-cut, bright pink tank top and black leather pants."

"What, you can't—"

"Two minutes and forty-five seconds," he quipped.

Again, Kisha clamped her mouth shut. She felt her body stiffen as she sorted quickly through a variety of spells. None seemed to fit.

"One minute and thirty-three seconds, Kisha."

His words snapped into her consciousness and she felt her stomach lurch. She wasn't going to make it. She'd end up standing in her pink bra and panties and he would unshield them.

Christine d'Abo & Renee Field

"Concentrate. It's within you. You have to trust yourself."

"Go f—"

"Forty seconds."

Kisha closed her eyes and prayed she'd get it right. *Pardus!* She let the word roll of her tongue and did a double take when she felt the cool feel of leather against her skin. She heard Foster clap his hands a moment before she felt brave enough to open her eyes.

"See, like I said, trust yourself."

He embraced her in a warm, tender hug that pulled at her heart strings. But that didn't mean she was happy with how he'd played her.

"You are such an arrogant—"

Kisha didn't have the chance to finish her sentence. Foster's lips claimed hers in a searing, heart-melting, toe-curling kiss that caused her womb to clench in sweet anticipation. His hands cupped her ass, so she reciprocated, yanking his tall, hard, lean body even closer to hers. Her breasts swelled as they rubbed up against his chest and she felt a trickle of desire seep onto her new panties.

He nudged her body back and pushed aside the low-cut pink tank top he had made her conjure so he could suck her nipples, leaving large wet stains on the satin bra. Not that she was complaining. Hell, if she could think straight, she'd zap off both their clothing. Then he moved his hand to rub her crotch, causing her to moan into his mouth and open her legs.

Kisha felt Foster stiffen a moment before she too heard the voices. She tried to ease his large frame off hers, but he stilled her, holding her cunt in place with his large hand. It was a highly erotic and dangerous situation for Kisha. She shifted slightly to keep her back off the books, now afraid she'd push one through to the other side of the shelf. He followed her actions with another harder rub over her now extremely sensitive mound. The tight fabric of the pink thong

Sweet and Spicy Spells

slid between her pussy lips, and with each pass of his hand, it added more friction to her achy clit.

"Listen," he said, whispering the word into her ear and then giving her lobe a nip, causing her to bite the inside of her mouth to stop mewing in delight.

She watched as he cocked his head to the side and then he lowered it, going straight to work on her still-wet nipple. This time he pushed down the shirt and bra, capturing her arms in the process.

"I said to stay still and be quiet," he admonished, while rubbing her mound with quicker strokes.

"There are people out there," said Kisha in the best quiet voice she could master.

"I know," he replied, moving his tongue from one engorged nipple to the other without missing a beat. There was no hesitation in his voice or actions.

Kisha had no idea the notion of having sex or the chance of getting caught in the act could be such a turn-on.

"Don't forget, quiet," Foster said a moment before she felt him will away her leather pants.

Goose bumps formed along her skin. She couldn't believe what was happening to her in the middle of a library, of all places. Make that the Archana Council library. Then reason fled. Foster palmed her ass, sliding his hands under the slip of thong fabric. His finger went straight to her greedy cunt, which was slick with yearning. She felt her inner muscles clench readily to receive whatever he gave. She parted her legs more for him and felt his body shudder. The entire time one hand played her wet pussy, his lips kept up their attention to her nipples. He pulled and nipped them, careful to keep his mouth quiet as he suckled them.

Okay, I can do this, thought Kisha, giving in to the desperate need to get rid of Foster's pants. She closed her eyes and concentrated on finding the correct spell. She mouthed the

59

words—*Patesco viscus*—and was rewarded with a long sigh from him.

"Sweetlips, you're getting good at this," said Foster, keeping Kisha's arms anchored in her shirt and bra as he moved to a kneeling position.

His intention was clear as day. She shivered at the wickedly erotic things he was doing to her body. Things no other man had ever done. Then again, thought Kisha, she'd never once in her slew of males had sex with a wizard. Even as she thought that, she knew in her heart that it wasn't the wizard he inherently was, it was simply Foster. He tuned in to what she needed. He demanded she comply because he knew she could. He trusted her when so many others simply laughed at her.

She felt him nibble at the triangle of satin and then his deft fingers pushed it aside so that the fabric was angled just so to rest on her highly sensitive nub. Damn the wizard, she thought, squirming with need.

"Put your leg over my shoulder," he said, as quiet as a mouse.

For a second, Kisha could have sworn that more people came into the room, but Foster was impatient. He grasped her right leg and positioned it the way he wanted…the way he demanded. Then his tongue was once again delving deep into her wet cunt. Her entire body shivered and her nipples puckered even more.

He's eating me. He's devouring me. Those two thoughts jumped into her mind. She yearned to anchor herself to him, but he kept her arms locked in the pink top he'd made her conjure. Then she felt two fingers slide deep into her opening. He pumped her hard, his fingers slamming into her even as he looked up and mouthed a reminder to be quiet.

Quiet? Kisha was so painfully aroused she no longer cared if she screamed out her pleasure. At the same time, she

Sweet and Spicy Spells

was also terrified she would inadvertently do something stupid like zap herself naked to a mall crowded with people.

"Trust yourself."

Foster's light whisper of words was a breath of fresh air on her sensitive nub. Then his tongue delved deep into her slick opening, forcing her to grip his head to steady herself. Kisha knew it was his way of forcing her to pay attention to him, her surroundings, the people on the other side of the bookshelf and her body that desperately yearned to climax.

Kisha felt him move the fabric of her thong out of his way. She felt him wet a finger with her own juices and then he slid it into her ass. The sensation was too much. He lapped at her pussy and finger fucked her ass over and over again. Kisha came so hard she trembled with the passion of release, her pussy pouring its liquid deep into his accommodating mouth. He sucked her dry and then tenderly removed his finger from her tight hole. He then proceeded to kiss his way up her body to her own lips.

She tasted herself on his mouth and it turned her on even more.

"Are they — ?"

"No." Foster moved her body around so that her back was to his front. "Can you be quiet a little longer?"

She nodded, understanding what he needed. It was also something she desperately wanted — the feel of his rock-hard cock buried deep within her. She felt him zap away the rest of their clothing. They were finally both naked. Both vulnerable. Both so hot with the need for sex they could fuel a dozen broomsticks on their own.

She felt his rigid cock rub between her open legs. He was lubricating it with her juices. She bent over slightly, providing him with the perfect angle. Again, he didn't hesitate. Foster grasped both her hips to anchor her in place and then plunged deep. For a second, she felt her body stiffen. His girth was wider than what her body was used to, but then she relaxed and her muscles opened up to accept his throbbing cock.

She heard his small groan of pleasure as he nipped her neck, attempting to keep quiet, and then he withdrew only to slide inch by inch back into her slick opening. He repeated the process painfully slow until Kisha thought she'd die unless he picked up the tempo.

I want him to fuck me hard. I want him to slam that cock of his deep inside of me. I want to feel his balls bounce between my legs. For a moment, she was shocked by the ferocious nature of her sexual appetite.

Kisha had always wanted a tender lover and that's what she had always gravitated toward. Now she knew she had been lying to herself. She wanted him to dominate her. Take her almost with force. She spread her legs wider, raising herself up on the balls of her feet. He pushed deeper into her and then his hand was on the front of her mound. She felt him gently move her wet lips apart and rub her still overly sensitive nub.

"Can you come again, quietly?" he teased the words into her right ear as he pulled his cock almost out of her pussy to only gently slide it back in.

"I need you to pound me." Kisha gulped. She couldn't believe she'd said that to him.

He hesitated. Then he licked her neck, the gesture oddly endearing and sensual as hell. "Kisha, sweetlips, when the time is right, I plan to fuck you so hard your knees will be raw. But for now, picture my cock pounding into your wet pussy, over and over again. Picture me tying you to that bed of yours and making you come until your clit hurts. That's it, sweetlips, let it happen. Fuck, you are so good," crooned Foster into Kisha's ear.

The words were so quiet, yet sensual, that Kisha didn't fight it when she came. She let it happen, again, reveling in the tremors tearing through her body inside and out. For a moment, when Kisha closed her eyes, she swore she saw a red

Sweet and Spicy Spells

haze. Almost giddy from the intensity of her climaxes, she tuned in to his need when he plunged deep, stifling his own groan into her hair. The hot spurt of his seed felt wonderful as her inner muscles milked his cock for all it was worth.

"So fucking sweet," groaned Foster, a moment before he slipped his shaft out of her wet opening and then very gentlemanly willed their bodies clothed. She was oddly moved by his considerate gesture.

"They're gone," he announced.

"What? When did that happen?" asked Kisha, wanting to get home.

"After you came the first time," he answered, a sexy grin spreading across his face.

Kisha punched him playfully in the gut. "You bastard. You did that on purpose."

He waggled an eyebrow at her. "You bet I did. But we've got a serious problem here."

"I know you can't help me. I'm doomed," Kish replied sadly, moving out of the tight confines of the bookshelf passageway.

"It's not you. Someone is trying to sabotage the Cup."

"What? How the hell do you know that?"

"The people outside. I caught part of their conversation."

Kisha spun around. *What? Why would anyone do that?* "I have to warn my sister."

"And I have to warn my brother."

Kisha's exhilarating mood evaporated. "Why do you have to warn your brother…just who is your brother, by the way?"

"Zack…oh, did I forget to mention my full name to you by chance? Sorry about that. I'm Foster Kane and Zack is my brother."

Kisha twirled and stormed out of the library, not even caring if she got caught. *Great, that's just great. Somehow I just know this is so not what my sister had in mind for me.*

63

Kisha knew things were only going to get ugly from here on in. The last wizard her sister wanted anything to do with was one Zack Kane. After all, every witch knew the Kane brothers left a trail of broken broomsticks and hearts whenever they landed in a witch's bed. Kisha vowed that most certainly was not going to happen to her. After all, if her sister could move on after being dumped by Zack and come to win the Cauldron Cup five straight years, it was the least she could do.

I might not be the best witch, but I will not let one Foster Kane win. So what if he can make me come…that's really no big deal. He will not win my heart!

It was a vow Kisha made to herself as she marched down the long formal staircase, not caring who spotted her or reported her to the council elders.

So much for a good day, thought Kisha. Sure, she had come for the first time in her life without her own fingers, but that was probably the last time. Already her body felt needy and achy with that thought. At least she could conjure her fantasy lover if need be. However, that thought didn't warm her at all anymore.

Kisha finally gave in to the urge to zap herself away. Away from him. Away from the prying ears and eyes of the council elders. Away from the only wizard who seemed to see the real witch she was deep inside and had not laughed at her. The only man who had asked her to trust herself. She fought hard not to sob, wishing Foster was anyone else's brother and not a Kane.

Sweet and Spicy Spells

Chapter Six

જી

"Winners always come out on top," Priscilla muttered as she cracked her fingers. "You can kiss my sweet ass, Zack Kane. *Deflagratio!*"

A metal bar that hung in midair in the center of the practice arena burst into flames. She'd been stewing ever since she'd poofed away from Zack's place after their little fuck on the floor. Why had she let things go that far? She was stronger than that, stronger than any man she'd ever been with in the past. But when it came to Zack, all her tricks didn't seem to work. Without even trying, he'd pushed past her defenses and set her emotions into a tailspin.

She'd tried to sleep last night, to put him out of her mind, she really had. But every time she'd closed her eyes and would start to drift off, images of Zack's naked body would appear, invading her dreams. Her body responded to the feel of his large hands squeezing her breasts, pinching her nipples just the way she liked it. Her body had hummed from the mind-blowing orgasms she'd had. Even now, her pussy grew wet at the thought of his large cock pounding into her.

To make matters worse, she'd heard his voice whispering in her ear. Telling her all the things she'd wanted him to say before he'd left her. Things she knew he didn't feel.

In the end, she got up this morning cranky, tired and in desperate need of another fuck.

"I won't be fucking you again any time soon, Zack Kane," she muttered.

Instead she settled for a little witchy workout. It was the only thing she could think of to calm herself down because there was no way in hell she was going to sleep with Zack

Christine d'Abo & Renee Field

again. If she never saw him again it would be too soon. Her heart couldn't take the beating.

Slowly, she walked across the open practice ring to the burning metal and tried to ignore the stench of sulfur and how it turned her stomach. He'd laughed at her when she began to hit him after his little comment. *Laughed!* He'd stopped when she started flinging pieces of his furniture against the walls. He didn't argue at all when she got to her feet and poofed out of there. Really, she was thankful he'd said it. For a moment, she'd had the silly misconception there might be something between them. She wasn't going to go down that road with him ever again.

"Stupid idiot," she said, not sure which of them she was referring to. "*Centonis.*"

The fire extinguished itself and the remains of the metal bar dropped to the floor with a thud. She stared at it for a long time and, for the first time in her life, felt completely deflated.

Zack was back.

Not just back in town, but suddenly back into her life—one she'd spent forever piecing back together when he'd left the first time. A tiny, mostly ignored part of her wanted to cry. She thought he had been in love with her long ago. Obviously he'd only been playing with her then, like he was now. She was stronger than that and she'd be dammed if she'd let him hurt her like that again.

Priscilla muttered a spell and a new metal bar rose from the ashes of the old one and hovered at eye level in front of her. When she heard the slow, steady rhythm of clapping come from behind her, she didn't even need to look around to know who it was.

She just couldn't catch a break, could she?

"What do you want, Zack? I have the arena booked for another thirty minutes."

"Not many wizards have mastered that spell, Prissy. I'm impressed. You did it without blinking."

66

Sweet and Spicy Spells

She had to fight the urge to gasp when she turned around to face him. He stood ten feet away, dressed in a black leather jacket, white dress shirt and black dress pants. His shirt was unbuttoned at the collar and she could see the tanned skin of his neck. His black hair was slicked back, like he'd just gotten out of the shower. Images of her lying on the floor, his cock pounding deep inside her, flashed through her mind again. Her body responded, her pussy growing damp as shivers of desire spread out from the center of her body. Ignoring the pounding of her heart, she rolled her eyes.

"If you're trying to figure out how to beat me, I'm keeping all my good spells under wraps."

Instead of a quick reply, Zack sauntered over to where she stood. He was sexy and knew it. Everything about the way he walked, the way he let his eyes roam over her body like a caress, oozed sex. It took every ounce of her self-control to keep from backing away as he approached. Her body betrayed her by responding, as a shiver of desire rolled through her. Why the hell did she let him get to her?

"*Evanesco*," he muttered, and the bar winked out of existence. The cocky smirk he'd worn only a moment ago slipped from his face. "We need to talk."

Priscilla felt her chest tighten, a lump forming in her throat. "I don't think we have anything to talk about. We had a good fuck, that's it."

His hand was out and on her arm when she tried to turn away. She felt a zing of electricity at the contact and her eyes flew to his. Zack felt it too. She could see it, the desire burning inside him, waiting for a chance to come out and play. She'd always loved that about him—his barely contained passion for everything in his life. She knew he never played, never laughed anymore. Not since the murder of his father. He'd idolized the older Kane and his death had taken a deep toll on the son.

That was why he'd had to choose between her and his job five years ago. It was the only way he had been able to search

67

Christine d'Abo & Renee Field

for his father's killer. But it had hurt so fucking much to come out on the losing end, even when she knew there wasn't another way. She turned her head, breaking the eye contact.

"Cilly, look at me."

"Don't you dare!" She jerked her arm out of his grasp, anger quickly replacing her self-doubt. "You lost the right to call me that a long time ago." She took a few steps away and stared at the wall of the arena. After a minute, she managed to get her breathing under control. "Why are you here?"

"I told you. We need to talk."

She turned her back to him and took a few steps away. She didn't want to look at him anymore. Wanted to freeze him out of her life, just like he'd cut her out of his.

"About what?" she muttered.

"Apparently more than I realized."

There was something in his voice that caught her off guard, tempting her. Before she could react, she felt him walk up behind her. Zack placed his hands on her shoulders and rubbed slowly down her arms, stopping at her wrists.

"Back at my place—"

"Forget it—"

"I didn't intend to hurt you—"

"I said forget it."

"I've tried to forget it, but thinking about it is driving me crazy."

Priscilla looked over her shoulder at him. She tried to ignore what his body heat and scent were doing to her and looked very closely at the man. For the first time, she realized he looked tired.

"I wish I could say I was sorry about your lack of sleep." *But I couldn't get you out of my mind either.*

"Is there somewhere we can go? I don't want to do this here." As he spoke, he ran his thumbs over the inside of each of her wrists.

Sweet and Spicy Spells

"What was the other reason you came here, Zack? I know it wasn't to talk about us."

Suddenly, he dropped her hands, allowing her to turn around to face him. She was scared by how quickly his expression changed from one of a passionate lover to the cold-as-ice warden.

"It's official council business," he said in a dead voice.

Every witch and wizard alike with half a brain in their head became nervous when they heard those words spoken aloud. Even the air between them seemed to chill for a moment. The Archana Council Elders ruled with an iron fist when it came to magic use, and the consequences for breaking the rules were painful.

They could take away the ability to use magic.

"Why the hell does the council want to see me? I haven't done anything wrong."

She knew he didn't buy her act of bravado. Zack gave her hand a squeeze, his eyes never leaving hers.

"Apparently, they've gotten word that you were using magic to influence people in the city. Not paying for items, making people forget you were there. But worse than that, they've accused you of harming people. Using black magic."

"What!"

"Cilly, they want me to arrest you," he said quietly.

No, no, no. This can't be happening. "Zack, I may be a lot of things. A bitch, high on myself, but I would never, *never* use black magic."

He didn't jump to her defense. Instead he slipped his fingers through hers and took a step closer. "You're so different from before. I admit some of those changes surprised me."

"You think I'm guilty," she said. The realization hit her like a sucker punch. Of all the people, she would have hoped Zack would know she wasn't capable of that sort of thing.

69

"Cilly—"

"No, that's it. You came here because you think I did it. You think I would hurt…" She swallowed hard but couldn't bring herself to finish the sentence.

Zack pulled her in for a hug. She stiffened, not wanting to take comfort in his embrace. He began to rub her back through the tight-fitting t-shirt she wore, his fingers digging deep. He made soft reassuring sounds as he kissed her temple and nuzzled her neck. Slowly, she felt her body responding to him. She leaned heavily against the solid wall of his chest. She rested her head on his shoulder and tried to block everything out.

"I don't believe them. If I did, you'd be under arrest and back before the council already. I think someone is trying to set you up."

Was he telling the truth? Probably, considering how seriously he took his job. Damn head of the council's security force. Lifting her head, she looked up into his eyes.

"I might be a pain in the ass, but I can't imagine anyone going to this much trouble to set me up."

"Unless you stepped into something far bigger than you realized. They may have realized that once you figured out what was going on, you'd make their life hell."

Zack smiled at her again and Priscilla felt her world melt away. She didn't want to react to him, to his warmth, but she couldn't help it. She felt her nipples tighten as a wave of lust washed through her. Her heart was pounding hard in her chest again and her pussy was damp. She wanted him bad.

"I make everyone's life hell. That's why most people run away from me," she said as she slid her hands around to caress his back under his jacket.

Zack raised an eyebrow and looked around at the ground. "I appear to be standing still at the moment."

"You weren't five years ago."

She felt the muscles in his arms tighten.

Sweet and Spicy Spells

"That was different."

Ignoring the sick feeling in her stomach, she simply shrugged. "Not really. You had us and your job, and then you only had your job. I didn't go anywhere, Zack."

When she tried to pull away, he wouldn't let her go. Priscilla could have easily cast a spell, not to hurt him, but enough of one to get her point across and to free herself. But she didn't. Now that she was back in his arms, that small, quiet part of her was starting to shout a little louder. And it wanted Zack back—desperately.

He slid his hand up her arm and across to grab her breast through her shirt. Priscilla bit her bottom lip to stifle a moan but kept her eyes fixed on his. His fingers found her nipple unerringly through the fabric and rolled it between his fingers.

"You know the type of job I have. What I do. I didn't want you being dragged into that."

Zack moved his other hand and pulled her shirt up to expose her breasts. His mouth latched on and began to tease her nipple, his tongue flicking back and forth until her body quaked. Priscilla fought desperately to keep control of her thoughts.

"Do I? I have no idea where you've been for the past five years, let alone what you've been doing. The last time I saw you was right before we were about to go on our date. And I don't think that turned out the way you planned."

"I planned on doing this." His words were hot against her wet nipple.

Standing to his full height, Zack kissed her hard. She sighed as she felt one arm circle her shoulders while his hand moved down the front of her body and into her pants. He dipped two fingers into her soaking pussy before parting her lips to circle her clit. Priscilla grabbed at his shoulders to try to keep her body steady.

"I wanted to fuck you so bad. To put my cock right here." He pushed his fingers deep into her cunt. "I don't know why

71

Christine d'Abo & Renee Field

we hadn't back then. It never seemed right. But now I know how perfect you are. I want you again, Cilly."

She was so close to coming, but his words jerked her back to reality. She reached down and put her hand on the part of his forearm above her waistband.

"Stop."

This time he listened and she pulled his hand out of her pants so she could move away. Her body was screaming its protest and she instantly missed the warmth from him, the intoxicating scent of his body that made her mouth water. But this was the right thing to do. She couldn't handle another disappointment. Not from Zack. More sex would only complicate things, and with this accusation on her head, she didn't need any further complications.

At least he had the decency to look as rattled as she felt.

"You should go," she said, and for the first time in her life she blushed.

"I can't," he said simply.

Right, his stupid fucking job.

"Look, I didn't do anything wrong. The council will figure that out and this whole thing will blow over. You're overreacting, Zack."

"I'm not the overreacting type."

Why did things always become so serious between them? She wasn't the brooding type, even if it did turn her on. She was Priscilla Morgan, Queen of the Cup. And it was about fucking time Zack learned that for himself. Priscilla blinked away her workout clothes and into her sexiest blue corset and a short black leather skirt. He didn't react, but she couldn't help but notice the growing bulge in his pants.

Taking a few steps away, she turned to face him and grinned. "I think this is just a ploy to throw me off. Find out what my spells are before you have to face me in the ring. Nervous, Zack?"

72

Sweet and Spicy Spells

Before she knew what he was doing, he'd shrugged off his jacket and begun to roll up his sleeves. A mix of mischief and grim determination blazed in his eyes.

"Let's do it," he said with a grin. "You've been boasting about how hot you are, Prissy. Time to put your spells where your mouth is."

No fucking way! She'd actually goaded him into a pissing match. Her heart began to pound again, but this time it was from anticipation. She was going to kick his ass. But she would have a little fun first.

"Please, if you think I'm going to tip my hand and show you anything before the Cup, you've got to be kidding," she said and added an eye roll for effect.

Priscilla crossed her arms over her chest and glared. But she wasn't going to let him off that easy. She felt the air between them begin to crackle and knew he was drawing his energy, getting ready to cast. Her body began to hum, the pull of such a powerful wizard charging her synapses to full. She still held back, wanting to push him into making the first move. Just to see if she could.

"I'm not doing it, Zack. Ouch!" *That didn't take long.*

A jolt of electricity zapped her ass in something akin to a pinch.

"Baby, I don't think you're up to the challenge."

She blinked and Zack stumbled forward from the little shove she gave him. "I'm up for any challenge you can throw at me."

Before she knew it, Zack had cast an energy ball at her. Priscilla had to dive and roll out of the way. She was on her feet for only a second when she sent a blast of wind at him and almost knocked him off his feet. Then something happened she didn't expect—she laughed.

"You should've seen the look on your face! I almost got you."

73

Christine d'Abo & Renee Field

Zack growled and ran straight at her. Before he got within arm's reach, she poofed away and appeared behind him. He wasn't easily fooled and she suddenly found herself trapped by an immobility spell.

"No fair," she ground out.

"All's fair in love and spell fights."

"There is no love between us." *Lust though. Definitely lust.*

Zack turned her around and released her from the spell only once he was able to touch her again. Priscilla shivered when she breathed in his potent musk scent she'd grown to love. Zack was panting just as hard from their spell casting and Priscilla found her gaze drawn to his mouth.

"You're stronger than I remember," he said and cupped her cheeks with his hands.

"I was always strong, Zack. You just never saw it."

She wasn't sure who initiated the kiss, but she wasn't about to stop it. Her mouth opened and she felt his tongue dip between her lips, coaxing her, licking the seam of her mouth, sending chills through her body. His hands were in her hair, coaxing her closer. Priscilla pressed hard against him, blocking all other thoughts except for him.

Their tongues sparred as her hands roamed over his body. She could feel the pull of his magic, the control not only over it but over himself. Priscilla wanted him to let go. Wanted to feel him pound into her without the restraint he showed back at his place.

She wanted him wild.

"Not here," he panted. "Somewhere else."

"You never wanted to fuck in public?" She reached down and grabbed his cock. "You *feel* ready."

"Cilly, you're driving me nuts."

From somewhere behind them, someone cleared their throat. Priscilla felt Zack suddenly move away from her as if she was on fire. They'd been burned, all right.

Sweet and Spicy Spells

"Isn't this an interesting picture?"

"Josh. This is unexpected," Zack said with a tone meant to scare the shit out of someone.

"I can see that. Ms. Morgan, I presume?" he asked, his eyebrows raised in mock surprise.

"Zack, aren't you going to introduce me to your *friend*?"

"Priscilla Morgan, please meet Josh Neil, my associate."

"Associate?"

"He means his partner. I'm a warden for the council too," Josh said and let his gaze travel down her body.

She didn't like the sound of distrust she heard in Zack's voice. The deadly looks passing between them weren't helping either. There was only one way she could play this—she was going to have to trust Zack.

"I can see you're the best of friends. What can we do to help you, Mr. Neil?"

Josh ignored her quip, instead turning his full attention toward Zack. "You should have brought her into custody by now, Kane. The council was wondering where the hell you'd gotten off to. Won't they be surprised to discover you've been kissing a fugitive."

"A fugitive?" Priscilla spun quickly around to face Zack. "You didn't say anything about me being a fugitive."

"I told you the council wanted to talk to you. You knew it was serious."

"*Talk to* is way different than *fugitive*."

"The council will have more than a few words to say to you as well," Josh spoke up.

Priscilla watched Zack's body tense before he turned around to fully face him. The air became alive with unspent power as the two wizards faced off.

"And why would they want to speak to me? Priscilla was about to pay her respects to the council. It's not my fault you were impatient."

Christine d'Abo & Renee Field

Josh smiled, or as close to a smile as Priscilla thought he could probably get. She should turn him into a rat. No, the rats would never forgive her.

"It's obvious you have a relationship with her. You should have told them that."

"First, my *relationships* are none of their concern. And second, they did know. That's why they sent me to talk to her and not you. Now if you don't mind."

When he finally turned back to her, Priscilla didn't know if she should be proud of him or pissed off the two of them had ignored her completely during their little interchange. She chose to keep her cool and gave him her best bored look.

"Priscilla Morgan, you must accompany me to the council chambers."

He held out her hand. This was the last thing she wanted to be doing right now, but she knew there was no choice. And despite being pissed off at him still, she'd much rather go with Zach than rat boy.

His hand was warm as she slipped her fingers into his. In a silent flash, they dematerialized, to reappear in the council's inner chamber. Only the highest members of the council and the wardens could gain entrance there. And all of them were currently staring at Priscilla and Zack.

The seven members of the council sat high above them dressed in yards of black velvet robes that covered them from head to toe. Their faces were barely visible, or would have been if there weren't a blinding light beating down on her, making it almost impossible to see. Priscilla snuck a glance at Zack. He stood calmly, his hands laced together behind his back.

"What now?" she whispered.

"Priscilla Marie Morgan." A booming voice filled the room.

76

Sweet and Spicy Spells

Shit. She felt the blood drain from her face and turn her stomach sick. *Fuck this!* She stood straight and stuck her chin out.

"Yes," she said and was thrilled her voice came out smooth and steady.

"You have been found guilty of performing black magic. What do you have to say for yourself?"

She swallowed down her nervousness. "I'm innocent, your honors. There has either been a misunderstanding, or I'm being set up."

"And why would anyone do that?" The voice seemed to come from all around her.

"I'm not sure. But it is the only explanation. May I see this evidence against me?"

"No. Take her."

"Council, may I speak?" Zack spoke up.

Priscilla's heart was pounding, but the fact Zack was here somehow reassured her. She'd get out of this. Hopefully all in one piece and with her magic intact.

"Mr. Kane, we are most displeased with you," the booming voice chastised. "This council trusted you."

"I've done nothing that would have you question that trust. But I do believe there is something wrong about this case against Ms. Morgan. I don't detect any hint that the black magic has touched her."

"Of course he wouldn't. He's been working with her."

Josh emerged from the shadows and Priscilla's mouth dropped. "You fucker, he isn't. And I haven't done anything wrong either."

"I found them kissing when I arrived to assist Zack with the arrest. I don't believe he can remain impartial."

"Agreed. Until we can make a determination, you are both under arrest."

"What?" Zack shouted.

77

Christine d'Abo & Renee Field

But before either of them could react, they were transported to a cell.

Chapter Seven

Talk about bad timing. Foster was pissed with what had happened. *And what did happen?* He was a wizard on a mission. He had fucked plenty of women and witches, but none like he had Kisha. None who made him want to be on his knees all day, licking her cotton-candied juices. None who made him push her buttons. None who made him giddy with a longing just to be near that unique chocolate chip cookie smell of her that seemed to instinctively comfort him.

She's just a mission. Just an assignment. Nothing more. So he told himself for the umpteenth time as he made his way through the cold halls of his home—Colard Castle. Foster cast a heat spell to warm up his body. *And just where the devil is everyone?*

Colard Castle looked like a typical German sixteenth-century castle because it was. The entire castle had been zapped in its entirety by his great-great-great-grandfather, who had a liking for striking a pose and loved to do things that started the locals talking. Not that it really mattered to a wizard, who had simply made all the locals think the castle had always been there.

Back then, the castle was rooted to the hundred acres of wild forest. Today the wild forest sat at the edge of the perimeter, and the property was made up of manicured lawns, a long white circular stone driveway and a huge rose garden on the left now greeted visitors. Inside the stone-lined walls hung tapestries rich in color and theme, all of which had been created through witchcraft by the Kane women. Besides the lush carpets lining the walls, beautiful, artistic antiques filled the rooms, adding warmth and luster that many said made

Christine d'Abo & Renee Field

Colard Castle unique. However none of that warmth greeted Foster.

After zapping back home, Foster had searched for any sign of someone. After all, the entire castle was home to at least a dozen wizard apprentices at any one time. A note fluttering at mid-height at the end of the hall next to the door that led to the kitchen finally caught Foster's eye.

He sighed. Great, he was alone for the night. All the apprentices were currently out on a seeking mission. It was the one mission a wizard had to complete working as a team. It had been the one mission Foster had hated with a vengeance.

On second thought, maybe my latest assignment is a blessing. Seeking missions always tended to be long, boring and dirty. And at the moment, the only dirty thoughts Foster was having centered around getting one Kisha Morgan naked, legs spread, arms tied high above her head. With that thought, he strolled to his private bedroom, knowing he had no way of talking to his brother until morning when the seeking mission was over. Then Foster planned to tell him everything he'd heard about the Cup. He just hoped he wasn't too late.

* * * * *

Waking from a restless night, Foster went straight to his brother's private study and poured himself a drink from the bar. To be precise, he poured himself his brother's best aged scotch, almost wishing his brother would materialize and yell at him for daring to touch his sacred alcohol. The liquid burned his throat and his gut clenched as the contents settled in his empty stomach. He'd have to get breakfast soon. The silence was interrupted by popping sounds as the wizard apprentices zapped back home.

Choosing to hold the amber tumbler in his hand just to taunt his brother, Foster went in search of the crew.

The sight that greeted him caused him to chuckle. Ten wizards stood in the front foyer, most either dripping wet or

Sweet and Spicy Spells

caked in mud from head to foot. All looked grumpy and Foster noted that not one of them cracked a smile at his laugh.

"Enjoy your seeking mission?"

"Shut the fuck up, Foster," spat Fergus, the red-haired giant in the group.

"And just where were you? Wuss," said Robby, the blond, blue-eyed wizard who was always looking for an excuse for a pissing match.

"Where I was, kid, doesn't concern you. But let me tell you it involved one hot red-haired witch, and while she wasn't as wet as all of you, she came big time," replied Foster, grinning. "Maybe you boys should all take a bath, warm up and call mommy to make you some cookies?"

"Foster, I'm warning you, shut up. You didn't spend the last ten fucking hours channeling the fucking sea, up to your armpits in stinking mud."

"Don't forget the fucking worms. I don't want to see another worm again in my life. Man, I think I've got fucking worms in my pants."

Foster stilled his chuckle. "Sorry, guys, that I missed out on that one. So where's my big brother?"

"Fuck knows," answered Robby.

"We thought he was with you," said Fergus, making his way to his room.

Foster's gut clenched again and it wasn't from the alcohol he'd consumed. Dread seeped into every pore of his being.

"Guys, are you serious? Zack didn't go with you on the seeking mission? He's been missing all night?" Foster downed the rest of his drink in one burning gulp.

"Honestly, we all assumed he was with you. Once we're all cleaned, we will help you look," said Fergus, who had stopped and walked back to the group.

"No. That's okay. I'll find him myself. You guys look exhausted. Go get clean and rest. I'll talk to you soon." Foster walked away from the group, headed back to his brother's study and poured himself a larger drink. He sat down in his brother's worn, brown leather chair, and then it hit him.

Of course, how stupid can you be, Foster? His brother was probably at Harry's Hideout, wreaking havoc all on his own.

Foster didn't hesitate. He zapped himself inside to the doormat of Harry's. The mat actually sat on the very threshold where the line had been drawn centuries ago. No magic in Harry's. It was the cardinal rule.

A second later, the door hit him in the ass and he spilled his drink. Turning furious eyes on the wizard, he gulped. It wasn't a wizard. It was a witch. And not any witch. Kisha. His witch.

Her umpf of surprise told him she was just as startled, however he couldn't seem to pry his eyes from the very wet stain now materializing on her shirt from his drink, which he'd inadvertently spilled on her when he had turned around. Foster was pleased to see it was the same low-cut pink shirt he'd made her conjure up in the library. The wet stain clearly outlined her large right breast and nipple. He ached to do the wizardly thing and zap it away, but he couldn't. The rule was simple. No magic at all.

"You're not supposed to be here. Leave," said Foster, more gruffly than he intended as he forced his eyes to move from her cleavage to his now empty glass.

"What, no sweetlips now, Foster? Get lost. I'm looking for my sister."

"There's a time and purpose for everything, Kisha. What do you mean you're looking for your sister?"

"You can be such an ass sometimes. I can't find Priscilla. She's missing."

"Missing," replied Foster.

"Nice echo you got happening there," snapped Kisha.

Foster watched as she turned away from him to make her way to the bar, all but ignoring him amidst the startled cries of

Sweet and Spicy Spells

protest coming from the wizards who viewed Harry's Hideout as their sacred nest. Witches were not welcome. Okay, the witch who won the Cauldron Cup was welcome, but no way was her sister.

Foster narrowed his eyes as two wizards got up from the back corner, making their way toward Kisha, who was now sitting pretty, dangling her feet on the barstool like she didn't have a care in the world while she used a black paper napkin to wipe off the alcohol he'd spilled on her breast.

If that isn't the most delicious sight. Foster watched as Kisha continued to dab uselessly at the stain. She looked vulnerable, slightly terrified and completely out of her element, he thought as she glanced at him. Then she turned her head away from where he stood. For a moment, Foster forgot to breathe.

He watched as Kisha released the tight ponytail from her flaming orange hair and coaxed her fingers through the mass to let it stream straight down to her ass. The mass of it was truly intoxicating. It was a like a beacon to every wizard in the place. He didn't like that at all.

Foster's nostrils flared as he caught Kisha's scent—vanilla and chocolate chip cookies. It took a lot of willpower, but he talked down his cock, which twitched with longing for just a wee taste of her.

"So, little witch, what brings you to Harry's? Looking for a good wizard to bang?" asked the first wizard as he leaned in on Kisha's space at the bar.

Foster fought the urge to move. Instinctively, he wanted to beat the crap out of the guy, but he was torn. His eyes scanned the crowded bar but there was still no sign of his brother. The only other place was upstairs. But Foster wasn't keen on the idea of leaving Kisha alone with a dozen horny wizards. Then again, with the mood he was currently in, maybe a good wizard fight would make him feel less on edge.

"You don't want him, little witch, you want me. I'm real big," said the second wizard as he stole the barstool to Kisha's right and had the audacity to brag about his cock for all to hear.

Thankfully, Kisha giggled. Surely they'd both take the hint and run with their tails between their legs, thought Foster.

Instead, the other wizard proceeded to put his lumberjack arm around Kisha's slender white shoulders, almost pulling her off the barstool in the process. Panic seized Foster's heart. *Surely she knew the rules. Surely her sister told her about the law.*

When a zap of bright yellow light flashed, he knew he was doomed. Lightning fast, he reached Kisha, a moment before all hell broke loose as every wizard in the place stood, demanding justice. Every wizard along with one ugly, warty toad.

"I can't believe you did that," groaned Foster, enjoying the ability to breathe the words onto the back of Kisha's neck while placing his hands on her shoulders.

She attempted to twist around on the barstool to glare at him. He stilled her actions.

"No thanks to you. And take your hands off me."

"Can't."

"What?"

"If I take my hands off you, then they will see us. More importantly, they will see you and then you'll be in prison."

"What are you talking about?"

Kisha tried again to twist her head over her shoulder so she could look at him. Foster knew if she turned, he'd see two hazel eyes full of fear staring back at him.

"The one golden rule at Harry's Hideout since the laying of the first stone is no magic. No magic at all. Anyone caught wielding magic is in violation of that rule and therefore turned over to the council. Anyone but Zack. He's usually the one enforcing the rules."

"You can't be serious. No one told me."

Sweet and Spicy Spells

Foster felt her slight shudder that vibrated like a taut wire throughout her slender body. "Is that going to be your defense, because it won't work. First off, no witches are allowed in—"

"But my sister goes all the time."

"Yes, but your sister won the Cup. The person who wins the Cauldron Cup can claim Harry's Hideout as their own with all the special privileges in tow," sneered Foster.

"Are you serious?"

"Yes. So I need you to zap both of us out of here now!"

Foster felt her stiffen and tremble at the same time.

"Aren't you afraid I'll zap us to the other side of the Earth?"

"I need you to zap us back to your place. And we have less than a minute before my invisibility spell wears off. Come on, sweetlips, you can do it. Trust me, you work best under pressure. Actually, you'd work best under me."

Foster couldn't help but grin. *Just where do I come up with these lines?* Only Kisha brought out the worst in him—or maybe it was the best part of him. He almost relished the strange situations he found himself in whenever he was with her. Maybe the strange feelings swirling around in the pit of his stomach had nothing to do with the fact that he'd been creeped out in his own castle or that he couldn't find his brother. Just maybe it was her.

"Are you serious? You want me to zap us specifically back to my place. The old farmhouse?"

Kisha's quivering voice broke his thoughts, zapping him back to their current predicament. He knew that freckled nose of hers was twitching, a nervous habit she wasn't aware of. A part of him ached to turn her around in his arms and kiss every freckle on her tiny, slightly upturned nose. But to do so meant the council wardens would surely find them. Another time, he promised himself, forcing her to keep still.

Christine d'Abo & Renee Field

"Twenty seconds, Kisha. It's now or never. I trust you completely," he said, leaning more into her still body.

He heard her mumble the words, and for a second he winced, thinking she'd said barn house, but when they materialized, they were back at her place.

He didn't want to take his hands off her shoulders, but she sashayed away from him quicker than a mouse could run from a cat.

"Okay, now you can leave." Kisha opened the red painted wooden door, which led straight into the old kitchen.

He knew she had no idea just how provocative she was. She stopped once she was safely inside the kitchen. The sweet scent of melted chocolate hit Foster's senses. From the corner of his eye, he watched as a large wooden spoon methodically stirred what had to be a batch of chocolate chip cookies in a huge ceramic bowl.

"I take it you like to bake?" He hoped she'd say yes because, boy, did he love a woman who could cook.

"What? I told you to get out. And yes, I like to bake. It makes me feel better."

Foster was stunned with that honest declaration. While he couldn't bake if his life depended on it, he certainly enjoyed home-baked cookies. Eating cookies had always made him feel safe, comfortable and, more importantly, loved.

It was the one thing he'd missed the most with the passing of his mother. She had been a great baker. There were always batches of chocolate chip cookies, macaroons, spider cookies and double-fudge chocolate brownies in the house. While she wasn't much into cooking meals, it never seemed to matter. Her sweet tooth was what had made his mother special. "Better a sweet wife than one who tastes like liver and onions." That had been his father's favorite saying when he'd swipe cookie batter from her bowl, hug her close and nuzzle the back of his mother's neck. She'd always smile and pat his bottom when she shooed him out of her kitchen. Much like

Sweet and Spicy Spells

Kisha, who was attempting to shoo him out of her kitchen. But all that changed five years ago with the brutal murder of his father.

"I said get out. Leave. I have to figure our where Priscilla is."

"And I have to find Zack."

"Zack is missing also?" asked Kisha, adding another cup of flour to the mixing bowl.

"Yes, nice coincidence happening there, don't you think?" asked Foster.

"You think they're missing together?"

Foster walked over to the cookie batter bowl and swiped a large handful for himself. *Real chocolate chips.* He couldn't help groaning and rolling his eyes in ecstasy. "Yes. We're going to work together and find my brother and your sister."

She walked over to the large white and black old-fashioned oven, peered inside and then took out a large baking tray without using any oven mitts. His stomach gurgled happily. Foster knew she had no idea that she was using magic, all without a second thought.

"I'm not working with you. I'll find her on my own."

He moved so that she came into direct contact with his hard frame. She tried hard to ignore him, but Foster felt her chest heave. "You do know you're using magic."

"What?" Kisha spun around and, in the process, almost dropped the hot cookie tray to the floor.

"Now that would have been a real shame," said Foster, moving past her so he could pluck the cookies he'd stopped in mid-fall from the air. He plopped two into his mouth for good measure. "There's something different about these ones."

"Belgian chocolate," replied Kisha. "It makes them sweeter."

"You know, I do believe you and I are going to get along famously. Now, as I was saying, we're going to work together

Christine d'Abo & Renee Field

and find our siblings," declared Foster, picking a large still-hot chocolate chip cookie so he could plunk it into Kisha's slightly open mouth.

She didn't hesitate to take his offering.

"These are even better than the ones my mom would bake."

She grabbed the rest of the cookies and placed them on a cooling tray. "Your mom baked? I'm having a hard time picturing the matriarch of the famed Kane clan anywhere near a kitchen," she said sarcastically.

He backed her into the kitchen corner, anchoring her by placing both of his arms on either side of her small frame. "My mom baked all the time. She was the best thing in my life," he said gruffly.

"I'm sorry, Foster. That was uncalled for. I didn't mean to make you upset," said Kisha. "I'm not usually that rude, you seem to bring out the worst in me."

"Maybe I bring out the best in you," he replied, grinning.

"I didn't say that."

"No, you didn't. I did," he said, a moment before he leaned his head down so he could lick the chocolate off the top of her lip. "At any other time, I would be thinking of a dozen delicious wicked things I could do with this melted chocolate…like licking it off your entire body, but sadly we can't. So any idea where your sister could be?"

"No. Any idea where your brother might be?"

"I tried the Castle, nothing. I tried Harry's and, well, you know they're not there. Usually I can feel his wizardly vibration…"

"Yeah, usually I can tap into Priscilla's, but it's like every time I try, I get blocked."

"Blocked? That's it. You're a genius," he said, a moment before he kissed her again, this time fully on the mouth, enjoying the sweet taste of chocolate coating her lips.

Sweet and Spicy Spells

She attempted to back out of the kiss, but Foster had another idea. He snaked his hands up her body and framed her head with his large fingers so he could angle her just so. She opened her lips, welcoming his tongue. The sweet taste of Belgian chocolate was like an aphrodisiac and images of him spreading chocolate all over her breasts flashed through his mind, firing his cock to its rigid position. A position he was becoming too accustomed to when he was around Kisha. Finally, Foster forced himself to stop and back away from the sweet temptation.

"They're in the council dungeon," said Foster, taking another step back so he could will control over his body.

"Prison! You can't be serious. Why would they be in prison? I bet your brother had a hand in this," said Kisha, sounding totally pissed off.

"Well, sweetlips, there's only one way to find out. Take my hand and let's be on our way."

"Wait," she said. A moment later, Foster watched spellbound as Kisha twirled her arms around, chanted some strange mumbo-jumbo and voilà, the kitchen was spotless, the cookies were all cooked and even neatly stacked on the cooling tray.

"Like I said, Kisha, you just need to trust yourself," he said with a chuckle.

She turned to him grinning. "I've always been able to use magic in the kitchen. Like I told you earlier, it's the one place that makes me feel comfortable."

"And like I told you, sweetlips, we are going to get along famously." He took her hand before she could protest and zapped them as deep as he could inside the Archana prison, known simply as the dungeon.

He couldn't zap them directly to any cell within the dungeon because that would alert the guards. Foster did manage to get them to the bottom level. They only had two

Christine d'Abo & Renee Field

more levels to descend to reach the dungeon, which was filled with at least a hundred cells.

"I really don't want to go down there," admitted Kisha.

He knew exactly how she felt, but they didn't have a choice. It was the only place where both their siblings could logically be.

"We don't have much time before someone spots us. We've got to move."

Foster grabbed her hand, forcing Kisha to follow him. He turned right and quickly found the steep stairwell that led to the remaining two levels. They had to descend single file and it was treacherous. The cold concrete steps got slicker as they descended. Foster felt Kisha behind him, cautiously watching her steps. A hundred steps. He counted that many as they reached the first of the two levels. He assumed they had to descend another hundred to reach the bottom, which would be completely devoid of any natural light whatsoever.

"That's the last level," he said, eyeing the cracked, crooked and even missing concrete steps that led the way to the dungeon.

"Lead on," declared Kisha. The nervous pitch in her voice betrayed her true feelings, but he was happy she'd mustered her courage to tell him to proceed. "Can't you make any light?"

"If I make light, they will see us," said Foster, almost sliding on his ass. He grasped the slimy stone wall for support. "Watch your step there."

"Got it. Thanks."

"We're almost there. Once we get to the last level, I'm going to have to use an invisibility spell," said Foster. "Hope it works."

"What does that mean?" she asked, the nervous pitch in her voice sounding more strained.

"I might not be able to use my magic."

Sweet and Spicy Spells

"What?" she squeaked and slipped at the same time, plowing straight into him, forcing him to his knees as he grasped the wall to halt their progress.

"Sorry," she mumbled, holding onto his back so she could stand up.

Foster attempted to stand and his left leg buckled. *Blast it! Once again the timing sucks. And why couldn't I have landed on my good knee?*

"Are you okay?"

"No." Foster forced himself to stand slowly, while attempting to put more weight on his right leg than his left. Task completed, he leaned against the damp stone wall. Sweat trickled down his back and he welcomed the cool feel of the stones. "Bad leg," he muttered, cursing silently in his head.

Two years ago, in the midst of tracking down a lead with information on who had murdered his father, Foster had given chase to an informant, only to leap over a fence and land flat on his left kneecap, shattering it. Even with surgery and the use of magic, it hadn't healed completely.

He felt her reach out to touch his back. Her delicate, tentative hand was soothing and exhilarating.

"Maybe we should go back."

"No. We're almost there. Trust me, we can do this," he said, with more conviction than he felt.

"Why do you keep saying that?"

"Saying what?"

"Trust me," she replied, her tone slightly breathless.

For a moment, Foster wondered if she was breathless because she recalled the last time he'd pushed her to "trust him" or because she had to continue to gingerly climb down the slick steps. "Because, sweetlips, I trust you more than you trust yourself."

"Nice oxymoron there," she snapped.

Christine d'Abo & Renee Field

"Actually, I think it's called the plain, simple truth," he said, his feet finally finding the dungeon floor. "There, we did it. Now all we have to do is search for them. They must be in one of the cells. Take my hand, Kisha. Let's pray this works."

He felt Kisha maneuver her hand into his as her feet finally touched down on the dungeon level also. Her hand was damp with sweat. Then he uttered the words he knew by heart and waited. When nothing happened, she stated the obvious.

"Guess it's not going to work. And we can't very well walk straight through without being caught within thirty seconds."

"Wait a sec," said Foster. He was trying to recall the time he and his brother had been able to link their magical powers together, binding themselves to each other to will a powerful spell. Just maybe he and Kisha could do that.

"Have you ever linked with your sister?" Foster hoped the answer was yes.

"Linked? What do you mean?"

"Well, I'm taking that as a no. Okay, we can do this together. My brother and I used to do this all the time," said Foster smoothly. *Talk about a downright lie.* "Let your thoughts flow freely into me and let the magic within you work with mine."

She stifled a giggle, but he heard it all the same. "Just where do you learn those lines? Let the magic within me work with yours. Yeah, baby, I totally understood that. And don't even think of uttering trust me, 'cause I don't."

"Okay, sweetlips, you got a better plan?"

"We talk to the animals here and ask them where our siblings are." She said it so matter-of-factly that he winced. Why the hell hadn't he thought of that?

"We can't use magic," he repeated.

"I don't have to. Watch."

92

Sweet and Spicy Spells

Foster watched as Kisha crouched down to the cold dirt floor and braced her hands palms down into the dirt. He heard her words like a rustling wind in his mind. Foster shook his head. *It can't be,* he thought, slightly awed. Kisha was asking the animals to come to her for help. She was speaking the universal language of the wild without a second thought.

Foster couldn't believe it. She had to be the most powerful witch he'd ever met. Sure, he'd heard the ancient legends of witches and wizards who could speak the universal language of the wild, but those had always been fanciful tales. No longer, as he watched four large rats scurry to her side. He couldn't help but shiver. *Rats! Why rats? Why couldn't she call forth a stray cat?*

"They know you don't like them. Don't be so rude, Foster," admonished Kisha.

"Well, it's not like I said I don't like them, but just to clarify, I don't. Couldn't find a cat to help you?"

Kisha ignored him. Foster thought he could discern what sounded like low chattering and realized she was deep in conversation with the rats.

"They are here. They're in one cell, together. It's at the end of the corridor. They say there's another way to get in. A hole."

"Yeah, I just bet there's a hole, about the size of my right toe. No way," said Foster.

"No, it's more like a tunnel, they say. I think we should trust them."

"Trust the rats. You are kidding, right?"

"Okay, Foster, you come up with a better plan, and guess what, two guards are heading this way, say the rats." Kisha delivered that bit of news too smugly for Foster's liking.

Foster quickly thought of his options. They all sucked. "Fine. Tell them to lead the way," he replied, grudgingly.

This time it was Kisha who led the way. By this time, he could hear the approach of the guards, who weren't bothering

Christine d'Abo & Renee Field

to be silent. *Well, why should they be? They're not trying to break someone out of the dungeon, which would make that a first.* Sadly, the idea of being the first wizard to break that rule didn't sit well with Foster, but like many things lately, he didn't have a choice.

"Here, behind this large stone," said Kisha, quickly stepping behind a large moveable stone that jutted slightly out of the wall.

Foster didn't hesitate. He followed her and the rats, feeling another one join them as it ran over his foot. His entire skin crawled.

"I didn't realize you were so prejudiced," said Kisha, ducking down now to crawl on her knees as the tunnel narrowed.

"Prejudiced? What, me? Can't a guy not like rats?," asked Foster, enjoying the view he had of Kisha's round bottom moving cat-like in front of him.

"Rats really aren't bad. In fact, my first familiar was a rat."

"Ahh, that explains it," teased Foster, ducking his head to avoid a tangle of old spider webs that netted across the tight confines of the tunnel.

"Explains what?" she asked.

"Nothing."

"What was your first familiar…or do wizards not have them?" she asked, crawling over a pile of stones that had caved in from the adjoining wall.

"Of course we have them," he snapped, knowing he was going to have spiders crawling all through his hair by the time this adventure was over.

"Well, what was it?"

"Nothing."

"Come on, Foster. I told you mine…you tell me yours," she teased.

Sweet and Spicy Spells

Her banter warmed his heart and soul. He was one hundred percent certain that no other witch who found herself in this current predicament would be teasing him.

"Fine, but you have to promise not to laugh," he demanded.

"Okay, I promise."

"Pinky swear."

"What?" she stopped crawling forward and twisted her head over her shoulder to look at him. "You can't be serious."

He nodded affirmatively.

"Okay, I pinky swear. And Foster, you had better not be lying to me, 'cause I will know. The rats will tell me. They can always tell when a person lies because their heart rate increases."

"Great, I really needed to learn that rats are living, breathing lie detectors. Okay, it was a cockatoo. There, I said it. Now let's proceed. My neck is getting cramped."

Thankfully, Kisha resumed her crawl. But he could have sworn he heard the rats laughing at him and that couldn't be a good sign, thought Foster.

"Was it white?"

"Was what white?"

"The cockatoo," Kisha asked.

Foster sighed. *I knew I shouldn't have said anything.* "Fine, you want the entire description?"

"Yup."

"Okay, the cockatoo was male, white with a bright yellow head. I named him Frisky, but he liked to be called Arnold. He had a thing for women's breasts. Hey, I told you no laughing. You pinky swore," said Foster, giving her ass a playful smack.

"Okay, sorry, you proceed. I just couldn't help it. Frisky? Please explain," she said, scurrying farther ahead, out of reach of his hand, which itched to slap her ass again.

Christine d'Abo & Renee Field

"First, do me a favor, ask those rat friends of yours if we're almost there, because my knee is killing me."

"Ooh, I totally forgot about your knee. They say we're halfway."

"Halfway. That's just great. Okay, the blasted cockatoo never listened to a word I would say. And just to clarify for you, that bird was always getting me in trouble."

"I can't imagine that," she said sweetly.

"You have no idea. He was always attempting to scurry up women's legs or sit on their shoulders so he could peek down their shirts. Or he'd nip their ass and then that blasted bird would yell my name, indicating I had done it. I can't tell you how many times I got reprimanded because of that little bugger."

"You know, you probably didn't treat it very nice," said Kisha.

"Treat it nice? The thing wouldn't let me come near it. It bit me so many times, I had to use magic to shield my hands."

"Well, you see, it was teaching you how to use your magic," said Kisha. "There. I see the opening up ahead."

Foster groaned loudly. "About bloody fucking time. As much as I like watching your ass waddle in front of me, I don't like crawling like a bug for what feels like eternity."

"Stop your whining," teased Kisha, poking her head out of the opening to ensure no one was around.

"Sweetlips, you are so going to regret saying that to me," said Foster, sliding closer to her so he could ensure it was safe to proceed. Once he was able to stand up, Foster made his move. *Heck, why not?* he thought, a moment before he pushed Kisha up against the cool stone wall and kissed her.

Her tongue snaked out to welcome his. Her arms didn't hesitate to climb his body, moving over his damp shirt, which was drenched in sweat and spider webs. With one leg, he nudged her legs apart and stepped in, while his hands moved to her ass, cupping her mound with relish. He squeezed both

Sweet and Spicy Spells

cheeks and rubbed his hard cock up against her belly. He caught her mew of delight deep in his mouth and that was when he heard the familiar sound they had been looking for.

"Foster, there's a time and place for everything," admonished his brother's voice.

The voice was coming directly across the hall from where he was making out with Kisha. He felt Kisha push him away from her and now she was blushing.

"Zack, get out of my way...before I make you."

"That's Priscilla. We found them," said Kisha, running past him to the large black metal door.

"So what's your plan for getting us out of here, Foster?" asked Zack in one of his bored tones that infuriated Foster to no end.

Foster moved to the door and peered inside the cell. "Well, you've finally decided to become a minimalist." Two single wooden beds, one on each side with only one worn cotton blanket, a small sink and an even smaller wooden table that held a pitcher of what he thought must be water made up their living quarters.

"Shut the fuck up and get us out of here. Now!" demanded Zack.

"Hoist me up, Foster. I want to see my sister," said Kisha, almost at the exact moment that Priscilla ordered Zack to move his large butt-ugly ass out of the way.

"I think I'm going to like Prissy," said Foster, watching as his brother muttered something under his breath and moved out of the way.

Foster grasped Kisha around her waist and lifted her up to the small barred window.

"Kis, what are you still doing with Foster?" asked Priscilla, staring past her sister to glare at him.

"You were the one who sent him to me...actually, he's not that bad."

Foster kissed the back of Kisha's head just to distract her. "Kis…umm, I like that a lot. And thank you, sweetlips," he whispered in her ear, blowing her hair out of the way.

"Cut that out," she squeaked.

"Lay a finger on my sister and I will turn you permanently into a toad," said Priscilla.

"I take back what I said earlier about her. And what's with you two witches and toads?"

"Less talk, more action. Get us out. The guards will be back shortly," said Zack, elbowing Prissy out of the way.

Foster dropped Kisha to the ground. She kicked him in the shin for that one. He was thankful it was his good leg. His other throbbed with each step he took.

"Okay, brother dear, what's your plan?" asked Foster.

"Prissy and I have something worked out. First thing, get the key ring that hangs at the end of the corridor," said Zack.

"The rats say they can get the key ring, no problem," said Kisha.

"Rats. What rats?" asked Zack.

"Cut it out with the rats, Kis. You know how I feel about them," said Priscilla.

Foster watched as Prissy and Zack jockeyed for position at the window.

"Well, that makes three of us, but if your sister thinks rats will help us get out of here, I'm all for it. Do it," said Zack.

"You heard him, do it," repeated Foster, moving away from the door.

He watched as once again Kisha knelt and placed her hands on the ground. He heard the answering chatter of rats and Prissy's squeal of surprise for what he could only surmise were rats now scurrying through their cell. A few minutes later, one particularly ugly, large and scarred rat ran up to Kisha with a shiny silver key in its mouth. He dropped it at her feet at the same time another rat dropped the ring of keys

98

Sweet and Spicy Spells

at Foster's feet. Out of the corner of Foster's eye, he watched as the large ugly rat bowed its head at Kisha. *Okay, I really must be losing it, unless she really is queen of the rats.*

Foster fought not to laugh at his own senseless humor.

"I've got it," said Kisha, picking up the silver key as Foster picked up the key ring.

Foster quickly found the right key, and with a twist and turn, the metal door swung open. Both Prissy and Zack stepped out. It was then Foster noted that each had silver shackles binding their hands.

"Kisha, you'll have to unlock us with that key. It's the manacles that keep us from using magic, blasted things," muttered Zack.

A moment later, both siblings were finally free.

Zack warmly embraced his brother, which Foster thought was highly unusual. His brother wasn't known for his loving character, but Foster wisely remained silent.

"So, in you two go," said Zack, pushing Foster into the cell.

Out of the corner of Foster's eye, he watched as Prissy ended her sisterly hug with Kisha and did the same. Foster had that sinking feeling in the pit of his stomach again.

"Is this your way of saying thanks, bro?" asked Foster, stepping more into the cell.

"Actually, this was my idea," said Prissy.

In the silence of the corridor, the metal door clicking shut sounded loud even to Foster's own ears.

"What's going on?" asked Kisha.

"Yeah, what's going on?" repeated Foster, feeling slightly foolish.

"The only way we'll be undetected and under the council's radar is if we switch places. So that's what we're going to do," said Prissy, now speaking through the window at Foster.

99

Christine d'Abo & Renee Field

"Not funny. Let us out, brother," demanded Foster.

"Can't. Prissy's right on this one. This is the only way. We'll try to make this quick. We'll be back by midnight tonight. In the meantime, why don't you and *Kis* work on channeling that magic of hers," said Zack, who had the nerve to actually wink at Foster through the barred window.

Foster growled. "You can't be serious."

"We are. Gotta run now. Oh, and don't forget to assume our identity. And you'll have to add the manacles for show when the guard comes by. Treat him nice, he's a real dear," said Prissy.

"This should only take a few hours, maybe a day at the most," replied Zack.

Then Zack and Prissy were gone. Zack's parting words felt like an arrow had been shot straight through to Foster's gut.

"That's just great. How are we supposed to assume their identity when we can't use our magic without the power letting the guards know something is up?" said Foster.

"I think now would be a good time to teach me that magic-link thingy you were talking about earlier."

Foster watched as Kisha plopped herself down on the small wooden bed.

She looked so sad and vulnerable, he fought against the injustice of what had just happened to them.

"That is the last time I ever save my brother's ass," he said, plunking down next to her.

"I'm in agreement with you on that one," answered Kisha as she turned her light hazel eyes up at him.

Then again, thought Foster, the idea of magically linking with Kisha certainly held many layers of appeal. He'd uncover all her secrets and all her fantasies. Knowing he looked like her fantasy lover made his cock throb with need. *Or maybe my cock just realized I'm sitting on a bed with a beautiful, tempting-as-sin*

100

Sweet and Spicy Spells

witch who amazingly still smells like chocolate chip cookies in the middle of a dungeon. How sad is that? All I can think of is sex when I should be thinking of how to escape.

Just then his eyes were drawn to the two iron manacles bracketed to the wall above the bed. He groaned loudly. Visions of stripping Kisha bare, placing her in those manacles and lapping her cream overwhelmed all common sense. Then again, nothing about Kisha was common. He hated the fact that eight pink glowing rat eyes were staring at him as if they read his intent. "Get rid of them."

"Only if you promise to behave yourself," teased Kisha.

There it was again. She was teasing him. Even faced with sitting in the dungeon, Kisha the witch didn't cave in.

Foster nodded, not trusting himself to speak. Once the rats left, he leaned over her, forcing her small frame to the bed. She gave one friendly, inviting squeal of surprise, but then circled her arms around his head to bring his lips closer to hers.

"Like I said, I promise to behave, *real bad*," he said, licking her lips.

"Somehow I just knew you were going to say that," she replied, hugging his frame closer to hers.

While this was the last place Foster thought he'd ever end up, especially with a wickedly enticing witch, a wizard couldn't be choosy. He'd been taught to make the most out of bad situations and what better way than to get their minds off where they were or what had happened to them by making love. He stilled.

When had it occurred to Foster that he'd stopped fucking Kisha and viewed their pleasure as making love? He wasn't sure when that had happened, but it had with a certainty that quickened his heart and fueled even more blood to the head of his cock.

"Kiss me again," moaned Kisha, tugging his head closer to hers.

101

Christine d'Abo & Renee Field

"Those sweet lips of yours are mine and I plan to wipe out every memory you have of another man's lips on yours, you got that, Kisha?" he said, nipping her lower lip.

She opened her eyes that were heated with need and stared at him. "Actions speak louder than words."

"So they do," he said, a moment before all common sense fled as he plunged his tongue deep into the heat of her mouth.

Sweet and Spicy Spells

Chapter Eight

ഔ

"Will you *move*! I can't see around you, you ape."

Priscilla shoved Foster—*Zack*—out of the way. He was blocking her access to the front door of Harry's Hideout. Why he'd insisted on coming this way instead of popping into the middle of the bar, she had no idea. Another giant shove gained her the same results—nothing. She couldn't move him at all despite throwing everything she had into it. She was definitely going to have to take Kisha to the gym after she got back into her body. The girl was in serious need of a workout.

Right now her emotions were a jumble and it was pissing her off that she couldn't straighten them out. She was still freaked out at the accusations against her, and she had to put a serious clamp on her wild imagination to block images of what the council would do to her. It didn't help that she was channeling Kisha either. Priscilla had no idea Zack made her sister nervous. Something else they were going to have to work on. *If* she could clear her name.

"Bit of a different perspective being down there, isn't it, *Kisha*?" Zack said and chuckled. "It's good to see how the other half lives."

Despite the mask of Foster's face staring back at her, she knew it was Zack. Even tapping into his brother's easygoing personality, Zack couldn't relax the way Foster could. He held his body ever so slightly different. There was an unmistakable spark that she recognized as his. It was the same spark that sent her body into overdrive every time he got close to her, every time he shot her one of those molten stares.

It made her want to fuck him senseless.

103

Christine d'Abo & Renee Field

"Look, let's get this figured out so we can drop the Kisha and Foster charade and look like ourselves again. I hate being short."

"You can't go charging into Harry's, *Kisha*. You're not the champ. Remember."

She felt the blush heat her cheeks. What the fuck was wrong with her? "Right. I knew that."

"Of course you did."

How the hell could she have forgotten something like that? Stupidity wasn't something she normally wallowed in. The link between her and Kisha must be throwing her off more than she realized. Had to be.

"Fine," she crossed her arms across her chest. "How do you propose we handle this? And me waiting outside is not an option."

Zack took another step forward and draped an arm around her neck. It felt awkward to be so much shorter than her normal height. It didn't help that he was able to overwhelm her not only physically but with his sex appeal. No wonder Kisha was drawn to Foster. In his own way, he was just as sexy as Zack.

But not the same.

"First, you need to stop acting like *Prissy* and start acting like *Kisha*. Your sister doesn't yell, get in a snit or generally make a pain in the ass of herself. She's quiet, smiles and listens. You need to learn some manners and behave."

"And how does *Foster* act? I'm sure he's not the bully you are," she snorted.

"Actually he's more of a hothead, but he has a better sense of humor. It's something I've always admired about him."

Priscilla looked up into his eyes and, for the first time since their reunion, saw something she hadn't noticed before. Zack was lonely. She knew it was loneliness because it was the same look she saw in the mirror every time she looked at

104

Sweet and Spicy Spells

herself. The realization felt very odd. Zack had always been the strong one—the one everybody could count on when they were in trouble. She'd never considered the fact that he didn't have anyone. Not since the death of his father.

That small, normally silent part of her mind wanted to say something to him. Wrap him up in a hug and tell him everything would be fine. But she couldn't do it. Fear of getting burned again was too much.

"I suppose you haven't had much to laugh about in the past five years, have you?" she said softly as a couple walked past them on the street.

Zack smiled, but it didn't quite reach his eyes. "The underside of society isn't the nicest place to live. It's a nightmare when you are there to clean it up."

"I was thinking about your father." She softened her voice.

He nodded once. "Both Foster and I tried, but we never caught the bastard. When Foster busted his knee, I knew we were both getting obsessive. I made him back off."

She was about to ask if he'd backed off when three very drunk wizards tumbled out of the bar, laughing and zapping each other with electric jolts.

"Shit, Foster, you should throw the runt back," one of the men barked and then stumbled past them down the street.

Priscilla's body tensed and she turned around to shout at them when Zack clamped his hand over her mouth. "Kisha would have ignored it. Look, let's get inside and get this over with. Think like your sister, bite your tongue and we just might get out of this in one piece. And remember, no spells."

She so wasn't in the mood for this.

"Okay, okay, let's get this over with. But when we're done, I'm going to kick that guy's ass."

Zack rolled his eyes and led her in the front door.

105

Christine d'Abo & Renee Field

Harry's Hideout had quite a different look when you had to come in the front door. Priscilla shoved her hands in her pockets as she looked around. It was harder than she thought it would be to put herself into Kisha's shoes. They'd always been close, but very different. As she looked around, she couldn't miss the nods to Zack and the eye rolls to her as they sauntered past the other wizards on their way to the bar. Is this what Kisha had to put up with every day? No wonder she wanted to stay at the farmhouse all the time.

"Foster," the bartender nodded, his eyes quickly landing on her. "I'm sure you're about to tell me why you brought your pet witch back here again. After the stunt she pulled, I'm tempted to lock her in the cold room and call the wardens."

"Again?" she whispered.

"Sorry about that, Jack. Kisha didn't know the rules. Don't worry, I gave her a spanking she won't forget anytime soon."

Jack gave Priscilla a long look and smiled when his gaze dipped to her breasts. "Yes, I bet you enjoyed that too, Foster."

"Back off, Jack, she's helping me with a problem," Zack said as he slipped onto one of the bar stools, resting his weight on his forearms against the bar.

Jack's eyes narrowed for a moment before chuckling. "Well, if she screws up again, she'll pay the price. No offense, but we can't have an inexperienced witch casting in this place. It's bad enough your sister pops in here as she does."

"You won't need to worry about me." She kept her voice calm and smiled, but inside she was seething.

"So what the hell is this problem of yours, Foster? I doubt there's much of anything I can help with."

"My brother's mentioned that from time to time…you hear things." Zack looked back at her for a moment before leaning in even closer to Jack. "Zack and Priscilla are being set up. The council has them."

106

Sweet and Spicy Spells

Jack's hands froze for a second as he was drying water from the inside of a glass. Nodding, he resumed his task, leaning in a bit closer himself.

"Well, that's certainly bad news for your brother. I take it you're looking for the bastards who did it?"

"My sister didn't do anything wrong. She's been wrongfully accused. Zack too," Priscilla said, taking a step closer to the bar.

It was funny, for a second she really did sound like Kisha. And it was more than using her sister's voice. She could feel her kindness, the lack of trust in her own abilities and the fact that she loved Priscilla. She had no idea Kisha felt so strongly about her.

Maybe that's why when Jack answered her, the full impact of what he said didn't hit her at first.

"No offense, but your sister's a right bitch. If it wasn't for the fact that Zack had been arrested too, I would have believed the charges against her. In fact, if you asked most of the wizards in here what they thought of her, they'd all agree."

"But we don't." The menace in Zack's voice was clear. "So you've heard about what's going on?"

"Shit, man. I'm being an ass. Sorry, miss."

"Forget it," Priscilla whispered.

"Jack?" Zack interrupted and drew Jack's attention back to him.

"I have. I think you need to take a closer look at some of your brother's past arrests. There was one guy who'd been getting in pretty deep with a gambling ring last time I heard. If both Prissy and Zack were taken out, I'd guess he's looking to fix the Cup."

Right bitch? Prissy? The smell of stale beer turned her stomach and Priscilla fought against the urge to gag. Her whole world began to spin and she wanted to get off the ride. She knew people thought she was cold, but she'd always thought Zack was the only one who called her that name. A

107

small barb to stick in her side because she pissed him off. But she didn't know this guy from a hole in the wall and that's what he was calling her.

Her normally sharp tongue lay silent in her head. Somehow she managed to swallow past the lump that had suddenly formed there. She couldn't focus on what they were saying anymore and instead concentrated on the steady movement of Jack drying the glass in his hands.

By the time Zack had finished talking to Jack, Priscilla was more than ready to return to her cell and never come out again. Not that she could let on at the moment. Would Kisha defend her? *Spells*, she didn't know anymore.

"Good luck with your test at the Cup tomorrow, Ms. Morgan. I'm sure Foster reset your system," he said and winked at her.

"How do you know about—?"

He chuckled. "I'm a bartender. I know everything."

"Time to go, Kisha." Zack tugged on her arm.

Priscilla nodded curtly and shot Jack a dirty look.

"Let's go check on Zack's recent arrests to see if any of them were released, Kisha. I'm sure the jailbirds are at each other's throats by now," Zack said and placed a kiss on her temple.

"Of course."

On their way out, Priscilla caught more whispers from the wizards.

"Can't cast her way out of—"

"Popped up naked—"

"Going to fail—"

Did Kisha have to put up with this shit all the time? Her face was blazing by the time they shoved their way past the front doors and out onto the street. No wonder Kisha lacked confidence. *Spells*, she'd probably made things ten times worse by suggesting she needed someone to help her. To even

Sweet and Spicy Spells

suggest *sex* was the answer proved how little she knew of her sister.

Priscilla knew she really was as bad as everyone thought.

"Next step is for us to find…are you okay?"

Zack spun her around to look directly at her. Despite the fact it was Foster's face and voice, she still saw him as Zack. For the first time in a very long time, Priscilla wanted to curl up in a ball and hide. Enjoy the warmth of another human being and stop being the tough one.

"I'm fine. Let's finish this so we can look like ourselves again."

"Cilly?" he whispered.

Priscilla yanked her arm away and marched down the street toward the alley they'd popped into with their arrival. Resting her head against the wall, she took a shaky breath and tried to get herself under control before Zack showed up. She didn't have to wait long for him to catch up to her. In a matter of seconds, he marched around the corner with a look that was a cross between anger and concern on his face. She stood up straight, ready to face him.

Not waiting for him to talk, she dropped the spell to look like herself again.

"What the hell is the matter with you?" he barked at her, looking over his shoulder to see if anyone had followed them.

"What's the matter?" she asked with enough sarcasm to freeze the sun. "Gee, Zack, could it have something to do with the fact I've been framed for something I haven't done and am now stuck looking like my sister, who apparently everyone thinks is a dork. Or maybe it's the fact that people seem to think me corrupt enough to use black magic and no one is willing to defend me."

"You need to ignore Jack. He's a prick and talks shit about everyone. That's what makes him a good informant." He ran his thumb over his lips and sighed. "I was hoping you hadn't heard the comments about Kisha."

109

Priscilla felt anger more at herself than at the wizards. "Coming to the realization that I royally fucked things up isn't a pleasant experience. I had no idea Kisha had to put up with all this shit."

"You didn't?"

He asked the question so softly she was almost able to ignore it. Almost.

"I did. She tried to tell me, but I ignored her. My instincts were completely wrong. I really am a self-absorbed bitch."

Her eyes were closed, so Priscilla jumped when Zack wrapped his arms around her. "You're not a bitch and I doubt there's anything wrong with your instincts. You've been going down the wrong path the last little while, that's all. And I have a feeling that might be my fault."

She saw the look of pain and regret on his face. Reaching up, she caressed his cheek. "I really missed you."

Zack winced. "I didn't want to drag you into that world. Shit, I didn't know if I would survive myself, let alone risking you. At the time, I thought I was doing the right thing. We'd catch our father's killer and things would be back to normal. In the end, you'd only be a little pissed at me and we would simply pick up and carry on where we'd left off."

He was trying to protect me? Even though this was typical Zack, it help fix the pain she'd felt in her heart for the past five years. It made sense, but it didn't reconcile with the pain she'd felt in her heart. She'd trusted him and was maybe more than a little in love with him. He'd taken that and crushed her.

The question now was whether she would let it ruin her life from this point on.

"I don't trust your bartender back there. Something was wrong," she said, taking a step away from him and the warmth of his arms.

"What do you mean, wrong? Jack's been an informant for years. His info has always been good," he said with a frown and crossed his arms across his chest.

Sweet and Spicy Spells

Priscilla couldn't help it, she rolled her eyes. "And who normally does the talking to your informant when you are trying to get information?"

"I..." he started, before giving his head a shake. "Josh."

"I bet it was Josh who first introduced you to him too. Not the most reliable guy, given our current situation."

Zack shook his head. "I guess I'm the one who should be questioning their instincts." He looked back down the alley at the pedestrians walking back and forth. After a minute, a slow, dangerous smile crossed his face. "We do have one advantage, though."

Instantly she knew. She could read it in every inch of his sexy body.

"They don't know it's us," she grinned back at him.

"They know Foster is a pretty decent wizard, but they are sure as hell not expecting you."

"What do you have in mind?"

Over the next five minutes, they hashed out a quick plan to get in there, grab Jack and get out. Once they had him alone, they'd be able to get the information they needed.

Zack turned, about to head down the alley, when Priscilla caught him by the arm.

He frowned. "What?"

"I'm not sure." She sighed. "I'm not sure if I have enough power to do this."

"Of course you do. You're damn near as strong a caster as I am. Maybe stronger with some spells," he winked.

A small part of her wanted to preen. He thought she was strong! Even so, she wasn't about to put either of them in jeopardy with a false act of bravado.

"Still, I'm creating a bubble that will haul us out of time. I'd rather have the backup and be sure."

Christine d'Abo & Renee Field

When he didn't respond, she took his hand and squeezed it lightly. "I'm not very good at asking for help. But I need you on this."

What she didn't expect was his sudden kiss. Her mouth was open as she gasped in surprise, only to quickly recover under the teasing caress of his tongue. She growled when his fingers found the sensitive spot on her neck, sending a jolt of desire straight to her clit.

Not wanting to be left behind, Priscilla slid her hand down his flat stomach and grabbed his cock, which was bulging in the front of his pants. Zack pulled his head back and Priscilla felt shock at the sight of Foster looking back down at her.

"This is too fucking weird," she said in a breathy voice.

"How's this?"

In a second, he dropped the spell and she watched Foster's green eyes transform into the rich brown depths that were Zack's. Funny enough, the size of the cock she held in her hands didn't change. Kane family legacy.

"Much better," she said as she pulled his face down for another kiss.

Her hands made their way inside his pants and she enjoyed the feeling of wrapping her fingers around his cock. Heat from his body wrapped around her and Priscilla responded to it, welcoming it. He was so long and thicker than any man she'd been with before. He fit her perfectly in so many ways.

"Zack, I need you."

He spun her around so she was facing the wall. Priscilla groaned, knowing what he was going to do, and wanting it now more than ever before. She braced her hands against the rough brick and wiggled her ass.

"Have I told you how hot I get just looking at your ass?" he asked, his voice coming in ragged breaths. She moaned when he squeezed her buttocks hard.

Sweet and Spicy Spells

"Shut up and fuck me."

He flipped her skirt up and yanked her thong aside. In one swift stroke, his cock was deep inside her, filling her to the top of her womb. He squeezed her hips hard as he began to move in and out of her with hard, even strokes.

"You wanted me to fuck you in public. Didn't you?"

"Yes," she moaned, not caring how it made her sound. She'd never been this turned on before.

"You like the thrill of getting caught. You want people to see your sweet ass, don't you?"

"Yes!"

Priscilla closed her eyes and let her chin drop to her chest. She felt invisible fingers stroking her inner thighs, teasing her clit. Her body began to shake with pleasure.

"So...fucking...hot," he said, punctuating each thrust.

"Zack," she moaned.

A very primal growl rolled out of him. "Say it again. Say my name."

"Zack."

"I want to feel your pussy squeeze my cock. Come for me, baby."

Her thong pulled tight across her clit, the rocking motion of their bodies added pressure. When Zack slid his hands up her back and around to cup her breasts, Priscilla thought she would die. He pinched her nipples, making her buck hard against him. Zack then leaned forward to suck her earlobe. All she could smell and feel was his body and wizard power. The sensations were everywhere, overwhelming her.

"Close," she whispered.

He dropped a hand to her clit, working her from the front with his hand as he fucked her from behind. It was all she could take. Priscilla's body tensed as she cried out, her orgasm racing through her. Zack never stopped and cried out, pounding hard into her as he came.

113

Christine d'Abo & Renee Field

They finally stilled, their pants echoing loud in the alley.

Zack brought his hand now covered with her juices to his mouth and licked her cream from it. "Hot and spicy. The way I like it."

They suddenly heard footsteps approaching the alley. In a flash, they both transformed into the images of their siblings with barely a moment to spare. A wizard from the bar had come to the alley to take a piss. When he saw them, he simply chuckled and went the other way.

"Nice ass." He slurred his words.

Priscilla felt her face heat as she stood up. She adjusted her clothing, but it took a little more effort to cover Kisha's larger breasts, pushing them back down into her corset.

Zack was watching her intently. It was strange seeing him as Foster so soon after what they'd done.

"I wonder if Foster minds you fucking Kisha," she said with a grin.

"If you breathe a word of this to Foster or Kisha, I'll arrest you again."

The look on his face was deadly serious, except for the twinkle in his eyes. Priscilla felt some of her old hurt start to melt away. She couldn't stop the grin on her face.

"Been there, done that." And she rolled her eyes.

He took a step closer and tugged up the front of her corset more. "Maybe I'll just spank you instead."

"Now that sounds enticing."

Zack sighed. "Are you ready?"

"Let's do this."

"Yes, ma'am."

Instead of entering the bar from the front, they snuck around to the back entrance. A normal human wouldn't even see the door, as it was protected with a conceal spell. It only took a single word for Zack to break through and let them slip inside unnoticed.

Sweet and Spicy Spells

Priscilla had to skirt around a precariously balanced stack of beer cartons in the dim light. They didn't dare speak for fear of drawing attention before they were set. Using hand signals, Zack motioned for her to hide in a small side room where the coffee maker and a small card table sat in the corner. There wasn't a lot of room, despite the fact she was in Kisha's smaller body. Thank the spells she wouldn't be here long.

She watched as Zack stayed in the shadows to the side, waiting for Jack to come back. They sat there a total of fifteen minutes before she finally heard his voice.

"Yes, sir. I'll be back in two shakes."

"Hello, Jack." Zack stepped out of the shadows the second the outside door closed. "We need to talk."

"Foster? What the hell are you doing back here? And where's your little friend?"

"I dumped her so we could have a chat. Is there something going on between Zack and Josh? And don't give me that shit about the Cup."

Priscilla watched as Jack looked over his shoulder toward the bar and then around the back of the storage room. She held her breath when his gaze passed over her, but he continued on without a second glance.

"Foster, you're too much like your brother. You need to learn to keep your nose out of other people's business. *Pulsus!*"

Jack sent Zack flying backward into the beer cases before he turned and bolted through the door leading to the bar.

"Zack?"

"Go! I'm coming."

Priscilla leaped after Jack and threw her body against the door. The light in the bar was far brighter than what it'd been out back. It took her a second to adjust before she saw him trying to exit the bar.

Christine d'Abo & Renee Field

"*Vicis Ebullio!*" she shouted the spell in the middle of the bar. All eyes were on her in the second before time stopped for everyone outside of the bubble she'd created.

Jack was still running but skidded to a stop at the edge of the bubble. He spun around and growled at her.

"I thought you were powerless, bitch!"

"No one ever said you were smart," she bit back.

"Too bad your boyfriend didn't make it in time to help you out."

She looked over her shoulder to see Zack frozen just outside of the bubble, his fingers mere inches from the edge. Jack took advantage of her distraction and fired an energy bolt at her. Priscilla barely had enough time to jump out of the way and roll to safety.

What Jack lacked in skill, he made up in brutality. Over and over he threw everything he had at Priscilla so she barely had time to get her bearings, let alone mount an offense. The burnt smell of spent spells filled the bubble, making Priscilla gag. It didn't help she wasn't used to Kisha's body either. Her legs weren't as strong, her reach shorter. Enough of a distraction to know she couldn't win this fight. Not alone at least.

With only a second to plan her next move, she rolled closer to Zack. "*Caecus!*"

Jack's hands flew to his eyes and he screamed in pain as she blinded him with white light. Hopefully it would give her enough time. Careful not to put too much of herself outside of the time bubble, she wrapped her hands around Zack's wrist and yanked him in with a loud grunt.

"You bitch!" Jack screamed.

Zack had to shake his head a few times, but she knew they didn't have time for him to adjust.

"Zack, I can't fight him and maintain the bubble. I need you now."

116

Sweet and Spicy Spells

"I can't...think yet." He squeezed her hand. "Take what you need."

Turning around, she saw Jack shaking off the effects of her last spell. "I'm going to rip you apart, you little whore."

The air within the bubble began to heat and sizzle as Jack began to chant a long spell. She suddenly realized it was black magic and knew this would be all over one way or the other in a matter of seconds.

She'd never linked with someone before and the sensation was odd. She could feel his power and a mixture of regret and pride. *You can do it, Cilly. Focus.* His voice echoed in her head, giving her the strength she needed.

Pulling energy from Zack, she went deep inside herself and found the one place in herself that was peaceful. She found her connection to the earth and all living things. She could feel Zack, feel his emotions rolling inside. Fear, love and anger all balled together and held under tight control. Calm passed through her body and into her soul, and for the first time in a very long time, Priscilla didn't feel alone.

Jack was practically shouting, his complex spell nearly done. She wasn't concerned. It was almost time.

Cilly?

She focused her attention squarely on Jack's voice box. As he was about to say the last line of the spell, she whispered, "*Sileo.*"

Nothing came out of his mouth. Jack's hands wrapped around this throat, squeezing, but it didn't matter. She'd taken a wizard's most powerful weapon—his voice.

"Nicely done." Zack squeezed her hand. "*Immobilize.*"

Jack's body froze in place, captured in a half turn trying to escape the time bubble.

"Are you okay?" She ran a hand over his cheek. "If I'd waited any longer, he would have gotten away.

117

Christine d'Abo & Renee Field

"I'm fine. But I don't think you will be, Jack. Even attempting to cast black magic is a crime, you know that. And seeing as we now have at least one additional suspect, *Zack* and *Priscilla* will be able to mount a defense now."

With a snap of her fingers, Priscilla let the time bubble fall away. They were instantly surrounded by the wizards in the bar.

"Holy shit!" someone from the back shouted.

"What the fuck is going on?"

"No fucking casting spells here!"

"Throw them out!"

"What's wrong with Jack?"

"Listen up," Zack shouted. Everyone in the bar instantly stopped talking and all eyes snapped to him. "Jack has been using black magic. He tried to cast it on Kisha and me in the bubble. He's going down for that, but I want to know what the *fuck* is going on."

Voices rumbled as the wizards talked to each other. Finally an older man stepped out of the crowd. Zack walked forward and they stepped to the side to talk. Priscilla kept her eyes on the rest of the group. Instead of the jeers and dismissive looks from earlier, she saw only respect. Maybe something good would come out of this after all. No one will mess with Kisha from now on. After a few minutes, she felt Zack's hand on her shoulder.

"I know what's going on. It's Josh."

"What?" Not that she was overly surprised, it still didn't make sense.

"We need to get back to the council now to warn them."

She looked at him from over her shoulder. "About what?"

"Josh is planning a coup. He's going to kill the council members at the Cauldron Cup."

Sweet and Spicy Spells

Chapter Nine

❧

Kisha knew what Foster intended, but she had her reasons for seeking sexual gratification. She just hoped she would be able to pull it off.

"Stop thinking, Kisha," admonished Foster as he moved to her right breast, kissing the already hard nipple through her shirt.

Abruptly, Kisha sat up, dislodging Foster in one quick movement. "I think I hear a guard."

"Guard?"

"Guard, Foster. Get your mind out of the gutter. That means we have to both flash into our siblings and behave like them. And don't forget the shackles. I don't think we have much time."

Kisha watched as Foster gathered himself. He stood tall and rugged in the small cell and then, in a blink, transformed into an exact duplicate of his brother Zack. The effect was slightly eerie yet tantalizing at the same time. By this time, she could hear the crunch of boots as the guard marched closer toward their cell. She felt her face flush and her heart accelerate as dread of being caught swamped her common sense.

"Sweetlips, like I've been saying, you always work best under pressure," said Foster, reaching out to lift her off the bed. "And let's not forget that Prissy charm of yours. It's now or never, Kisha."

The jangle of keys told Kisha the guard was almost on top of them.

"You know you can do it. Trust yourself."

Christine d'Abo & Renee Field

Boy, did Kisha hate it when Foster said that, especially when he said it looking like Zack with those chocolate brown eyes of his when she longed to see the comfort of Foster's clear emerald-green ones.

Trust myself. Of course I trust myself. Kisha wrinkled her nose at him.

"Reach out with your magic and link with your sister. You not only need to look like Priscilla, but you will need to talk and act like her."

For a moment, Kisha wondered if Foster was playing her, but she had to admit that he sounded like his brother and the commanding no-nonsense tone of his voice was no longer playful. More abrupt and to the point.

"Kisha, it's now —"

"Shut up!" she said. Kisha closed her eyes and forced a calm she didn't feel. Then she reached out, seeking the thread of magic that was unique to her sister. A second later she grasped it, held it tight and instinctively bound it to herself, claiming a part of her sister with it. For a moment, she could have sworn she heard her sister shout "no" in her head, but Kisha quickly shook that off.

"My, my, my, your sister is really beautiful," said Foster, a little too quickly for Kisha's liking.

What did she expect? She knew first-hand she didn't look like the average witch, let alone act like one. Still though, Foster's comment bothered her. Then it dawned on Kisha just as the guard turned the key in the slot that she felt more confident, more in control and way more sexy than she had ever felt in her life. *Maybe role-playing will be fun.*

She turned her body, remembering at the last moment to zap shackles onto her wrists as a guard walked into the room, carrying what Kisha surmised was their breakfast.

"About bloody well time," she said, turning to look at the guard.

Sweet and Spicy Spells

"Sorry about that. There was a problem in the kitchen, but I brought you your favorite," he mumbled, blushing and staring straight at her with desire fueling his eyes.

Kisha caught herself. *So this is how my sister feels. Powerful. Beautiful. And sexy as sin. The complete witch package.* Kisha knew then that her sister had this one particular guard eating out of her hands. She blinked, realizing in that moment the guard wasn't really staring at her, he was looking at the person he thought she was, her sister.

Kisha decided it was time to up that charm of Priscilla's. She sauntered over to the guard, took the tray from his arms, handed it to Foster without a word and then turned back to the guard, who had turned an even darker shade of red.

"Thank you, I really do appreciate —"

"All you've done for us," interrupted Foster.

Kisha twisted her head around and couldn't help gulp. He stared straight past her and eyed the guard, all but making the poor wizard tremble. A tic had started in his jaw and the deep dark chocolate brown of Zack's eyes were almost black with fury.

"Zack, I left a message for your brother," said the guard quickly, all but groveling at the mighty wizard's feet.

Kisha was pissed, or was that the emotion her sister would feel. She didn't like the power Foster, now Zack, was wielding one bit. She strode closer to the guard, fingered his dark gray jacket and tilted his head up to hers. *Wow, height does have its advantages.* Kisha loved being able to tower over someone for a change.

"I think I promised you more than just a thank you," she said, taking delight in watching as the young wizard's eyes opened wider in surprise. Kisha yanked the guard to her now tall body, making sure to press her breasts into his chest and kissed the poor guard senseless. She felt his battle for a second, but then he was kissing her back with relish. Kisha felt Foster yank her out of the guard's embrace before the guard's tongue found its target. She was pleased the guard had missed out on that opportunity.

"Get out. Now!" yelled Foster.

The guard, now beet red and realizing what he had done, didn't hesitate. He scurried out of the small cell faster than the rats had.

"Sorry, Zack. I don't know what came over me," he said, safe from the other side of the metal door, which he'd remembered to click shut behind him.

A moment later, the scrunch of the guard's boots running down the corridor could be heard by both of them.

Kisha whirled to confront Foster while zapping the pretend shackles away. She desperately wished he had turned back into his original self. She much preferred Foster's emerald eyes to Zack's hard, cold brown ones. Before she could say anything, he backed her toward the bed on the other side of the room, forcing her legs to move of their own accord. With her sister's height, she was almost as tall as Zack.

Kisha was about to yell at him when he grasped her body and hoisted her on top of the bed. Then he shoved her wrists inside the two iron manacles hanging from chains on the wall next to the bed. Two swift clicks followed. Her heart jumped straight into overdrive.

"So you want to play a Prissy game...well, let's get to it," said Foster, a moment before he undid the top button on her black leather pants and yanked them without any fanfare down to her ankles. He pulled them off like an expert.

Kisha shivered. The feral gleam in Foster's eyes was startling her. "Maybe this magical link isn't such a good idea, Foster," she squeaked.

He ignored her and ripped her thong from her bottom. With her black corset still on and her bottom half naked, she felt more exposed than if she was completely in the buff.

"Enough. Cut it out, Foster!"

"That's not what your sister would say," he teased.

Sweet and Spicy Spells

"I'm not my sister. *Verto tergum!*" Kisha said the words and a second later she was back to her original self, minus the clothing Foster had torn off her. Too bad the spell didn't seem to do anything to the manacles or clothing, she thought, hating the disadvantage in height now. She was forced to stand on her toes to not feel the pull of the manacles and already her arms ached. She cursed inside her head, hating that she had also forgotten to clothe herself.

She heard Foster's sigh as his fingers crept up to the insides of her bare thighs. His featherlight touch made her stomach clench in sweet anticipation.

"Much better," he said, his head moving closer to her belly.

"Okay, your turn," she said, giving a yank to the manacles. They barely budged.

"Make me," he taunted, a moment before he ripped open the front of her corset, exposing her breasts.

"I can't believe you did that," she squealed, wishing she could cover herself.

"Spread your legs," he ordered.

"No. I'm not doing this. I can't do this. It's too weird…"

Foster yanked her legs apart on the bed. Her feet dug into the old wooden frame, but she stood straight.

"You'll do it and like it, but it's up to you when I change. And if you continue to disobey me, I will have to punish you."

Kisha really wished he sounded like Foster. She couldn't tell if he was being his playful self with that rough, commanding baritone voice of Zack's, which demanded, never enticed. A strange part of her also relished the erotic role-playing, which made her feel vulnerable and sexy at the same time.

"I see I will have to give you a demonstration."

Just what does my sister see in him? Kisha had to admit Zack's physique was very similar to Foster's. They both

123

obviously worked out, but as demanding as Foster was with her, none of it hit her on the same level as Zack's commanding tone. It was Foster's playful, teasing banter that made him unique, that along with his eyes which seemed to see deep within her heart and soul.

What am I thinking? Kisha shook her head, trying hard to clear her thoughts. She had made a vow earlier that no Kane brother was going to leave her with a broken heart like they had her sister. *No way,* she reminded herself.

Before she could further protest, Foster turned her around, twisting the chains together, exposing her bottom to his gaze. He slapped both of her ass cheeks hard, the sting cutting yet strangely exhilarating. No one had ever done that to her before. No one had ever dared or wanted to. Then she felt Foster's lips kissing the sting away. She almost wished he wouldn't stop.

"Are you ready to follow my commands?" he asked, twisting her back around to the front to face him.

She desperately wanted that face to be Foster's, not Zack's. As if he read her mind, he said, "It's up to you to transform me."

"I've been trying. My magic isn't strong enough," she snapped.

"You're enjoying this. And here I was thinking you were drooling over my dark, brooding looks."

"This isn't funny anymore, Foster. Transform!"

"No, Kisha, it isn't funny. Make me, sweetlips. Or just maybe you like the idea of my brother with his face buried in your pussy. Don't make a sound."

"Cut it out," she squealed, but it didn't matter. Foster was no longer listening to her. He nudged her legs apart, forcing them into a wider stance, and then he buried his face in her mound, lapping her cunt with his tongue. She shivered as the sounds of him licking her reverberated in the small cell. She fought to stifle a moan, but it was no good.

Sweet and Spicy Spells

"I heard that," he said, lifting his now glistening face out of her crotch.

Like before, he turned her around, twisting the chains that held her arms apart. She braced herself for the feel of his hand on her ass. When nothing immediately happened, she twisted her face around to look at him. He was on his knees. He'd removed his pants, freeing his throbbing erection, which he now held in his hands. *Wow, guess the brothers do share some big family traits,* thought Kisha, trying hard to stifle a giggle.

"Transform me, Kisha."

It was a ragged plea she heard in his rough voice. She closed her eyes and fought with herself, seeking the right transformation spell. When she found it, she mumbled the words. Nothing happened. "I can't."

"More like won't," he said, a moment before he smacked first her right ass cheek and then her left. Her bottom burned. Sexual tension filled the air.

"You like that my brother is going to fuck you…you witch," he snarled, even as he kissed and nipped his painful smacks away.

Kisha tossed her head. His erotic words caused her puckered nipples to tighten even more. *No, I don't. I don't want Zack.* She fought for a hold on the magic, wishing with all her might she could wield it to transform Foster back to his original self.

Kisha stilled as Foster's hand worked her wet mound, his fingers dipping into her tight opening only to slide out and then move to the crack of her ass. She fought not to squirm with need. Then his tongue licked the crack of her ass. She moaned loudly, the sensation strange, yet sexually titillating.

She felt him back away. Felt the cool air of the cell. It was a stark reminder of their current situation and she couldn't believe she was allowing him to do this to her. But she was. That was the bottom line. She knew instinctively Foster would never hurt her. He might be angry with her and he might push

125

Christine d'Abo & Renee Field

her buttons to the limit, but he would never harm her. Never do anything she didn't really want. And that was it. She wanted this. Wanted him to take her like this — his captive, his witch slave. She shivered, finally giving in to the role she was forced to play.

"Say you want me," he demanded, blowing hot air through her legs, causing her to rise up on her tiptoes.

"No," she rasped out, biting the inside of her cheek for clarity.

He leveled a sharp, small smack to her still-smarting bottom. Kisha groaned loudly. He followed his action by smacking her other cheek lightly and then he turned his hand around and smacked her cheeks between her legs, almost but not quite hitting that sensitive part of her that yearned for it. Again, like before, he tenderly licked and kissed the red blotches away.

"On your knees," he said, pulling the manacles with brute force from the wall to force her down to her knees, but keeping her backside to him.

She wondered what he wanted.

"You're going to make yourself come, like this," he demanded.

Of all things she wanted to change, it was Zack's voice the most. She closed her eyes and focused.

"Do it."

Kisha couldn't believe her ears. She had to be sure.

"Do what?" she asked, innocently.

"Sweetlips, play with yourself," he said.

The sweet, teasing voice of Foster filled the cell and her head. *I did it.* She had at least gotten the right voice she wanted to be pleasuring her and Kisha knew it was only a matter of time before she found the right spell that would transform Foster back to his original handsome self. She just hoped that was before his cock found its way into her wet cunt.

126

Sweet and Spicy Spells

She felt his hands nudge her bent legs apart more. He slid a hand over her glistening cunt, turning his hand so that his fingers found her opening. He dipped in for a moment and then withdrew and once again slid it along her cheeks.

"Do it, Kisha," he said.

Kisha closed her eyes. *Just how the hell does he expect me to play with myself if my hands are still held in place by the manacles?*

"I know you can conjure up the feel of your hands, so do it, 'cause, sweetlips, I'm not letting you loose," he said, leaning his body over hers, forcing her knees to take more of his weight.

The heat of his body and feel of his chest hairs on her naked back sent tremors of need to ripple through her body, while her brain desperately wanted to tell him to go to hell.

"This is for your own good," he said, licking the inside of her right ear and then moving to her left. He twirled his tongue along the tender nerves of her earlobe and then sucked on first one, then the other. She shivered as goose bumps formed along her flesh.

"My own good, that's a good one," she repeated, hating how breathless she sounded.

"Think of me as your lucky charm."

Kisha was about to say something else, but all thought left her when he moved his hands to her two heaving breasts and tweaked the nipples hard. Then he rubbed them between two fingers and repeated the action. Pain and pleasure spiked through every nerve ending in her body.

"Trust yourself," he said, moving her long hair off her neck so he could cascade kisses down her neck, down her spine and suck on the underside of her bottom cheeks. It was so tender, yet so erotic she leaned forward, providing him with better access to her cunt.

"If you play with yourself. I'll play with you also," he said, his voice light, but gruff, with desire at the same time.

127

Christine d'Abo & Renee Field

Kisha closed her eyes, yanking her arms to see if they'd slip through the manacles. *No dice.* So she thought deep and imagined her own fingers playing with her nub. At first it was a light brush she thought she'd imagined, but then an invisible finger tweaked her clit, causing it to pebble hard, and she groaned loudly. At the same time, she felt Foster's fingers work her from behind. He'd slip one finger into her slick pussy and then move it to coat the crack of her ass.

She continued the assault on her pussy and even managed to imagine her own fingers tweaking her nipples as hard as she liked. It almost felt like there were three people working her body into a state of sexual gratification she'd never experienced before, but it was only her and Foster.

Only her using magic. Only her trusting herself. Only Kisha trusting the wizard loving her while pushing her own buttons at the same time. She wondered about that, but then she felt Foster's wet finger push at the tight hole of her ass even as her own invisible fingers continued to rub her nub in tighter circles. Then he pushed first one finger and then two deep into her ass. The violation of it. The pleasure of it fired her magic and she felt the connection—that magical link he'd talked about.

She felt Foster, knew his secrets, knew his desire to prove that she was a powerful witch and, more importantly, she felt her sister through the link. She knew her like never before. Knew what fired her sister to compete, knew how insecure she really was about herself and then all reasoning fled. She felt Foster angle her and then the hard tip of the head of his cock was at her wet opening.

"I want you, Foster," she said, moaning the words loudly in the cell.

"I'm going to take you every way I want," said Foster, and somehow Kisha knew she'd managed to transform him. It wasn't the façade of Zack fucking her anymore. It was Foster Kane making love to her. Making her feel treasured. Making her trust herself.

128

Sweet and Spicy Spells

His cock rammed her deep and she mewled in delight with the feel of the tip almost touching her womb. He withdrew slowly and then plunged back in. She squirmed back, wishing she could get rid of the manacles that held her wrists, because she longed to be on her hands and knees with him pounding into her from behind. It was almost animalistic, the urge she felt to be dominated by him. And then before she could blink she heard the click as the manacles magically released her. She bowed down to the bed, bracing herself on her hands, willing him to plunge even deeper, even faster into her.

He completely covered her. His hard, lean, muscular body draped hers, forcing her to collapse to the bed. He didn't withdraw. He somehow managed to stay tight within her. She felt his towering presence from behind, felt him adjust so that he was on his knees. She kept her ass slightly raised off the bed making it easier for him to plunge that cock of his deep inside of her. She felt his hands mold and squeeze her ass cheeks and then he was picking up the tempo, riding her with long hard strokes that caused her face to rub roughly into the worn blanket covering the bed.

One of his hands hauled her slightly up and she didn't hesitate. Her own hand found her wet nub and she tweaked it in time with his strokes and then she felt his fingers back in her ass. He was filling her. Filling all of her. With every stroke of his cock, he'd simultaneously plunge his fingers into her tight hole, forcing her to relax and release her breath at the same time. The sensation was too much. Kisha felt the edge of the climax coming and then, before she had time to force the feeling away, she was over the cliff, taking Foster with her as he plunged deep, held himself in place, his hot seed shooting deep into her clutching pussy.

He slowly withdrew, turning her over at the same time. Kisha opened her eyes, loving the intense reflection of Foster's emerald-green eyes as they looked at her with such tenderness.

Christine d'Abo & Renee Field

"You are the most powerful witch I have ever met," he said, claiming her lips before she could thank him. Then again, making love to him again would be thanks, she thought, loving that his wet cock was already twitching and growing with longing for her.

* * * * *

"I see when the cats are away the mice will play," said Priscilla's voice through the metal door.

"About time," said Foster, moving from the bed to the door. "Is everything okay on your end?"

"The council elders have cleared us for now. I'll fill you in later, but basically the council believes we're innocent. Not that you seem to care, brother. Looks like you really were enjoying your assignment," quipped Zack as he opened the metal cell door to release them.

Kisha blushed as she inadvertently remembered all the things Foster had done to her when he had transformed into Zack.

"So, is she fixed?" asked Zack to Foster.

Fixed? Assignment? "You bastard, Foster. Get out!" shouted Kisha, flying off the bed without realizing it.

"Stop yelling. He did fix you," admonished her sister.

With one powerful zap from Priscilla's fingers, clothing appeared on Kisha and Foster.

In her rage, Kisha had forgotten she was naked. Realizing what she had done caused Kisha's anger to reassert itself even as she blushed bright red with embarrassment.

But Kisha would not be swayed. She had just realized Foster Kane was a true Kane in every since of the word. A bastard who left her heart breaking and it was a good thing she didn't have her broomstick because she was certain she'd use it to bash his grinning face in.

Sweet and Spicy Spells

"Get out, everyone. *Absentis!*" shouted Kisha without thought, zapping them all away, even her sister.

But it didn't take her sister long to flash back. "Good to know you're in top-notch form, Kis. It's time."

"Time?"

"Time for you to face the council." Priscilla reached out to take Kisha's hand, giving it a slight squeeze. "I'm really proud of you. I've always been."

Where is this coming from? wondered Kisha. Her sister wasn't icy with her, but she also wasn't one to share her feelings. Then Kisha knew. It was because of the magical link they'd formed. They each had stepped into the other's shoes and gotten a taste, a different perspective of what life was like for the other.

"And I've always been proud of you," said Kisha, returning her sister's squeeze.

"Good. Now it's time."

Kisha had completely forgotten about the test. Her heart felt as if it had plunged to her feet. She felt her sister give her fingers another slight squeeze, which released the surge of magic she felt spiraling through her head.

She nodded, wondering at that moment just where she had zapped the Kane brothers to.

"Don't worry, they'll be okay, once they get themselves out of the pigsty," chuckled her sister.

"Oh no, tell me I didn't."

"Oh yes, you most certainly did. Nice thoughts you must have been having of Foster," quipped her sister, a moment before Kisha felt herself being zapped from the dungeon.

Christine d'Abo & Renee Field

Chapter Ten

❧

"Are we inside what I think we're inside of?" asked Kisha. Her heart was still reeling with the spell her sister used to transport them away from the dungeon to the front steps of Colard Castle. It was dark and the sky was bright, filled with the expanse of stars. The old castle was eerie, yet at the same time, with the darkness engulfing them, it was beautiful.

"Yup, we're about to enter the infamous Colard Castle—home to the Kane family for the past several hundred years. I'm sure Zack could give you a precise date, but I'm not interested. So, are you ready for this, Kis?" asked Priscilla, giving her a once-over.

Then Kisha watched as her sister smiled. A real, genuine smile that relaxed her harsh expression and made her look lovelier, almost softer.

"Yeah, you're ready. So, I think you've got some secrets you'll want to share with your big sister when we're done here," said Priscilla, winking at her as she moved her along the long, dark corridor.

Kisha felt her face heat in embarrassment, knowing exactly what special secrets her sister wanted to hear. Desperate to change the topic, Kisha asked the obvious. "So you and Zack figured out who set the two of you up, right?"

"Yes, Zack's old partner. But we can't prove it yet and the council won't move to arrest him until we can. Our plan is to force Josh to show his hand tonight."

Kisha almost stumbled as her sister opened the door, ushering them both inside. "Tell me you're not using me as bait, please."

"Okay, we're not using you as bait."

132

Sweet and Spicy Spells

"But you are, right?"

Abruptly, her sister halted. "Just to set the record straight, this was not my idea."

"That's right, it was mine," said Zack, materializing to Kisha's right, causing her to gasp. In the process, she almost knocked over what looked like an original Ming vase.

Kisha watched as Zack barely blinked, halting the vase from smashing to the floor. Zack Kane didn't look like he had spent the last few minutes face down in a pigsty. He looked every inch the wizard warrior he was. Dressed entirely in black, with his dark wavy hair brushed off his face and his brown eyes heated in anger, he looked ready to kill. *I just hope he's not looking to kill me*, thought Kisha, moving away from his presence only to bump into another solid form she was all too familiar with, as the fresh scent of pine mixed with that musky masculine scent slammed hard into her.

He might not be looking to kill you, but I'm certainly going to punish you for that one, sweetlips, said Foster, his deep rumbling voice vibrating in her head straight to her toes. Kisha gulped.

How? How is this possible? Fear fisted itself around her accelerating heart as she heard his chuckle float through her subconscious.

You tell her, Foster.

Kisha turned her eyes to look at Zack because that was Zack's voice she heard this time inside her head. She didn't like Zack's devilish grin one bit.

Okay, that's enough, you two idiots. It's because of the shared magical link you formed with us, said her sister's voice loud and clear in her head. That almost scared her more than hearing Foster's and Zack's.

And Kisha, only a really powerful witch can form a magical link like you did, so relax. Everything will be all right.

"All right? No, it won't. Everyone stop right now. I can't take all of you talking in my head. I don't like it one bit," she said, her cheeks now bright pink in fury.

133

Christine d'Abo & Renee Field

"It's okay, Kisha, you will adjust to it. And trust me, it can come in handy. However, we can explain all of this to you at another more appropriate time. The clock has almost chimed midnight and we need to present you to the council now," said Zack.

There was no mistaking the commanding tone in Zack's voice.

"Yeah, sweetlips, let's get this show on the road," echoed Foster.

For the first time, Kisha really looked at Foster. Dressed now in black leather pants and a matching black shirt, he looked sinister and sexy. The combination was gut-wrenching in its effect. Then he winked at her, giving her a look that said he could read her mind, as he placed his arm around her waist, drawing her to him. She felt his comforting heat and instantly felt more powerful, more relaxed and confident.

"I'll be here for you. And like I keep saying—"

"Trust myself," said Kisha, finally understanding why he had pushed her buttons.

"Zack, would you and Priscilla walk ahead? There's something I need to say to Kisha," said Foster.

Kisha watched as Zack nodded, wizardly understanding lighting his eyes as he grasped Priscilla around the waist. For a moment, Kisha waited for her sister to push him away. However, she did the opposite. She leaned her tall frame more into Zack's powerful body and together they ambled down the long corridor as close together as possible. It was a sight Kisha thought she'd never see—her sister leaning on Zack for support.

Don't get all mushy on me, Kis. I'm still the bad one, said her sister's voice inside her head.

Kisha simply nodded a moment before Foster spun her around so that she faced him chest to chest.

"Just so we're clear on a few things. One, you are going to pay for that little stunt. Two, you might have started out as a

134

Sweet and Spicy Spells

wizard assignment, but things changed. I love that you don't always get it right. I love that you aren't afraid to make mistakes. I love that you're adventurous. I love the mind-blowing sex we have and I love you."

"What?" squeaked Kisha.

"You heard me, so don't play coy with me."

"But you can't. I'm not at all the type of witch your parents would ever have approved of."

Kisha felt Foster pull her closer to him so her chest was now crushed into his. She felt his fingers tilt her chin up so that she was now staring into his emerald eyes that almost vibrated with light.

"My parents would more than approve of you. That's what I've come to realize about you. You make me feel comfortable. You make me remember. Remember what it was like when they were together. And for the love of everything, you smell like chocolate chip cookies, always."

Kisha tried to pull away. "Foster, I'm flattered, but it's not going to work. I'm not sure I'll even get my witch status after tonight."

"You will."

"Seriously, I'm always making mistakes."

"But you're not afraid to try. So what if you make mistakes. So what if you don't always get it right. So what if I end up face down in a pigsty, again—"

"I really didn't mean for that to happen."

He padded her bottom lip. She stilled and felt her eyes close with that surge of desire she always felt around him. "I'm glad it did."

Kisha couldn't believe her ears.

"That was the first time in my entire life I've ever seen anyone get the better of my brother and, trust me, his totally mortified look as he realized what you did was worth it. Now, sweetlips, we do have to go, but I plan to make sure you

135

Christine d'Abo & Renee Field

believe what I said," said Foster, a moment before his lips descended and claimed hers.

Kisha wrapped her arms around his head, hugging his hard frame to hers. Their tongues dueled with longing, but it was Foster who was the first to pull back, slightly panting.

"Now, sweetlips, let's show the council how powerful you really are," he said, lacing his fingers through hers.

Kisha felt the surge of his power easily flow into her and when next she opened her eyes they were standing in what had to be the inside glass-covered courtyard. She shivered.

I know exactly how you feel. Trust me, this is not normal. Our home used to feel warm and inviting, but the last time I was here I felt like this. And I've got a feeling by the end of the night we will know why.

Foster's words were meant to reassure her, but they didn't. A thousand questions flitted through her mind. Why would anyone want to sabotage the Cup? Who is behind it? And just how did Colard Castle tie into it all?

Before she could ponder anything further, a cloud of purple smoke scented with the sharp tang of jasmine filled the courtyard. Then a soft-spoken voice addressed her.

"Kisha Jollymore Morgan, you have been brought forward to the council elders to perform the three tests necessary to approve your witch status. You understand that you must perform the three tests independently and that you must pass all three. If you fail to pass all three, we will erase the knowledge of magic within you. Do you accept the terms?"

"I accept," answered Kisha, fighting for a breath.

Kisha wished she'd taken at least two breaths, because when next she looked, she was standing on a mountain, at the edge of a cliff. She had a sinking feeling it was the sacred Mount Everest.

The first is a test of physical strength. The second is a twist and turn to tweak the mind, and the third involves changing potential time elements in history, which is always

Sweet and Spicy Spells

the scariest thing to cast. Every witch and wizard knew the rules. Only one spell could be used for each test.

"Help me," said a weak voice from below the cliff.

It took a lot of nerve for Kisha to peer down. Vertigo set in fast. She closed her eyes against it and stepped back, feeling her feet slip on the snow-covered precipice.

Trust yourself.

She blinked. Foster's warm voice of encouragement calmed her. She wondered for a moment if that was allowed but wasn't about to question it.

"I'm slipping. Help me!" screamed the man's voice.

Kisha inched forward on her hands and knees. There, barely holding on to a yellow coiled rope was a young man, no older than her. His fingers, clad in climbing gloves, were beginning to slip through the rope that kept him from falling to his death.

"Help me!" he screamed again. "I can't hold on much longer."

Kisha didn't know what to do, but she knew this test was real. *If I fail, he will die.* That cold knowledge propelled her to gather her courage. Her eyes spied the end of the rope that connected the man sprawled over the side to the top of the mountain. She knew she'd never be able to haul him up as she was, but that didn't mean she couldn't do it. She grasped the taut rope, barely managing to pull it up enough so she could tie it around her waist.

Verto iam! The spell flew through her mind, transforming her body instantly. She started to move her sure-footed goat feet and grunted under the full force of the man's weight. The process was painfully slow. Her shoulders strained to haul the man to safety. Just when she thought she couldn't trudge another step, she felt the rope relax and heard the man grasp the edge of the cliff with his own hands.

"Well done, Kisha. Didn't like the idea of dying at all," said the man, zapping into his original wizard form.

137

Without thought, Kisha transformed back into her original self. *I should have known better.*

"Test one, completed. Passed," said a loud booming voice coming from the air.

A moment later Kisha found herself zapped somewhere else. She was flying through the sky, spiraling fast to the ground, wishing she'd remembered to pack her broomstick, or an elastic to keep her hair from whipping around her face.

Call the broomstick to you.

Like always, Foster's voice reassured her. The soft brush of his words whispered the confidence and trust in herself she lacked. But Kisha knew there was no way her broomstick would make it in time. And she couldn't transform again, she'd already used that spell.

Call it to you, now!

"*Iamo virga!*" Kisha shouted the words into the whirl of the wind whipping around her body, which was dive-bombing toward the ground, fast. *There is no way it will make it here in time,* she thought. Panic welled up deep inside her.

"*Verto iamo virga no alestico!*" Kisha shouted the words as a desperate plea, not sure if they would work, but what the hell. A trill sound coming from below forced Kisha to look down. Sure enough, someone's broomstick was zooming straight for her. About five hundred feet from the hard ground, Kisha grabbed hold of the broomstick, thankful it could at least hold her weight. She angled her body to the side so she could sit on the broomstick and then promptly forced it to land. Once her feet were safely on the ground, she used the opportunity to wipe the sweat from her brow, tucking her wild hair behind her ears.

"I thought I was a goner," she said to no one in particular.

"So did I," echoed Foster, materializing next to her only to sweep Kisha into his arms and kiss her senseless.

Kisha struggled. "What are you doing? This is an infraction of the rules. You've got to go. I only have one more

Sweet and Spicy Spells

test and then I pass," said Kisha with a lot more conviction in her voice than she felt.

"I don't think I can watch another test," replied Foster, still not releasing her.

"Watch? I thought this was between me and the council elders?"

"Sorry about that slip. I shouldn't have told you that, but don't worry —"

Then Foster was zapped away before he could finish his sentence and Kisha stumbled, barely catching herself before she fell flat on her ass.

"Test two complete. Passed," said a loud council elder voice.

Everyone is watching me. I can't believe it. I can't do this. Those were her last thoughts before she found herself being zapped back in time, ending up once again at the dungeon. This time, though, she had been transformed into a rat. *Poetic justice,* thought Kisha.

Kisha heard a loud groan coming from a cell up ahead and decided to investigate. She scurried on her rat legs and easily climbed the metal door to squeeze her agile body through the small cell window, which had thick steel bars. There before her was the last person she'd ever thought to see—Magnus Kane, Foster and Zack's father, Head of the Wizard Wardens since long before she was born.

Kisha wouldn't have recognized him, except that the guard who was zapping him seemed to enjoy using his name.

"This one, Magnus, is for that demotion you threw my way last year," said the guard, chuckling evilly as he leveled a deadly blast at the old man.

From what Kisha could see, Magnus had been kept in the dungeon for some time. The pungent odor of soiled clothing and unwashed bodies assaulted her sensitive rat nose. She judged by the multiple shades of colors from the bruises on his face and body, which was barely covered in thread-bare

139

clothing, that Magnus had been in the cell for at least a couple of months.

"Just get it over with, Josh," said Magnus through clenched teeth, falling to the cold, hard cell floor.

"Why? I'm having such fun and I plan to have a lot more. My plan is so easy, it's devilish."

"That's the black magic talking," croaked Magnus, bracing his upper body with one arm resting on the cold floor.

"Well, old man, you're right about that. Black magic, white magic, and let's not forget that illustrious red magic no one talks about anymore."

"It's forbidden," whispered Magnus, his head bowed down to rest on his chest.

"Thankfully, I'm not the forgiving type." Another zap followed and this time the rat Kisha had transformed into smelled the acrid, coppery scent of fresh blood.

"When I'm done, your sons will never think it could have been me. Me, Zack's most trusted friend, Foster's mate and all-time party-going pal. Me. The one who has absorbed all I can from you, old man. Your time has expired. And soon so will the entire Kane family," taunted Josh, firing a volley of powerful zaps at Magnus who no longer fought them off.

"My only regret, old man, is that you won't see my final act of sabotage because I honestly believe a father should be proud of what his son achieves." Those parting words were the last Josh said as he aimed a deadly zap directly at Magnus' chest.

Kisha heard Magnus attempt to take a ragged breath in and then he collapsed to the ground. Josh didn't so much as register a flicker of emotion on his face as he zapped himself out of the cell.

What am I supposed to do? What do they want me to do? Kisha's sensitive hearing heard the scrape of hundreds of rats scurrying to the cell. She knew exactly what the rats would do to Magnus and she couldn't allow it. Even as she thought how

Sweet and Spicy Spells

best to stop the army of rats advancing, she rehashed the conversation she'd overhead.

Could it be true? Was Josh Neil really using black magic and was he really the son of Magnus, a brother to Zack and Foster? And what is he really after? He hadn't hesitated to murder Magnus after he'd absorbed all the magic from him, but to what end? And what is red magic?

Those thoughts jumped into her subconscious even as Kisha fought to transform back into her original self. No go. The council elders had transformed her into a rat and she wasn't able to undo their spell. A dozen red gleaming eyes glared hungrily at her. She huffed up her fur to make herself look bigger than usual and prayed she could still communicate with the animals. She pleaded with them, chittering away until she felt the connection. One by one, they bowed their heads at her and departed. When she was at last alone, she turned her attention to Magnus and stilled. He was still breathing, just barely.

"Tell my boys, will you," he whispered to her, his eyes flicking open for less than a fraction of a second.

Then Kisha understood. Even though Josh had somehow absorbed Magnus' magic, Magnus could talk to the wild like herself. He had heard her plea to the other rats and was using his last breath to ensure she told the truth.

"What can I do?" she asked, chittering away like a rat.

"There is nothing you can do. Josh must be stopped. It's bad enough that he's using black magic, but if he finds out how to use red magic, we will never be able to stop him. Ever. For all time. Tell my boys I love them," said Magnus, a ragged breath barely escaping him.

Kisha fumed at what she was witnessing. *I will not let this happen.* She sorted through all the spells she knew to find a way to make things right. And then an idea sprung to life. One life for another. Could she do it? Would it work? What did she have to lose?

141

She called the nearest rat to her without thought. The large rat entered, staring at her. *Vita pro vita!* She spat the words out fast like a rat, but forced the magic within her to work. A strange tingle started to raise the bristling hairs on her body and then a red haze filled the small cell. When next she blinked, still in rat form, Magnus was dead. *Or was he?* Kisha forced herself to pay attention to the large rat standing in front of her.

"Magnus?" she asked, praying it would be so.

"Yes," he chittered, slowly lifting first his right and then left legs.

Kisha watched as Magnus the rat slowly turned, trying to get used to his new body.

That was the last thing Kisha saw before she was zapped back before the council elders.

"Test three. Passed," said a council elder.

Kisha was overjoyed to pass the test, but she had more important news to tell the council elders. They had zapped her back in time to make things right. *The third test had to mean something,* she told herself.

They knew. The council elders know. Everyone had watched it. But was it real? Kisha was at a loss. She felt drained like never before.

A moment before a bright zap almost took her head off, a strange red haze filtered out around her to form a protective bubble where she stood. Kisha was thankful the shield held, but she had to tell them what she'd learned. She had to tell Foster and Zack. She had to make them understand.

And what the heck is happening out there? she wondered, unable to see anything through the red haze that was saving her ass, but obscuring her vision of what was taking place. She could hear what sounded like a battle, but things like that didn't happen in front of the elders. *Or do they?*

Sweet and Spicy Spells

Chapter Eleven

ॐ

Zack leaned back against the wall and said a silent prayer to the cosmos that Kisha would pass her test. He could see the change in his brother tonight when they'd pulled themselves out of the pigsty. Foster had smiled and laughed at the fact she'd dumped him there. Something had happened between them over the past two days and he liked the difference he saw in Foster. Seeing what Kisha had done for his brother also helped take the sting out of Zack's *very* undignified landing. He'd never be able to wear those clothes again.

Zack closed his eyes and enjoyed the rush of adrenaline he always got before a big arrest. Every nerve of his body was on fire, ready to jump into action. Tonight he was going to put Josh away for good.

Priscilla sighed and switched her attention to a second bag she'd blinked to herself. She was currently decked out in black leather pants, a corset and bent over right in front of him. She really did have the nicest ass he'd seen in years. Nothing against Kisha, but he was happy to have Priscilla back as herself. At least *she* didn't dump him in a pile of shit. Not yet at least.

Besides, he planned on fucking her senseless after this was all done.

"Did you find it yet, Prissy? We really need to get going if we're going to catch Josh in action."

She turned her head to look up at him from over her shoulder. "You're the one who said we won't have time to get back here before the Cup and I'm not going without it."

Her long black hair swung in the air, framing her face, and her painted red lips pouted at him. She was so much more

143

Christine d'Abo & Renee Field

relaxed now that Kisha had gotten a grip on her spell-casting abilities. She probably felt the same way about Kisha that he felt about Foster. Part sibling, part parent. She only wanted the very best for her sister. He knew she really wanted to be there with her right now, but the council insisted they take care of Josh before the Cup. Kisha would be okay— Foster would see to it.

When she winked at him, he realized there was something else different with her. The sparkle in her eyes knocked the wind out of him. She was happy. The coldness was gone and she looked truly happy. At that moment, Zack realized how much he'd missed her. Missed the kidding and teasing and even their occasional fights. *Okay, more than occasional.* When this thing with Josh was resolved he was going to do something about this, about them. The very thought of which got his heart pumping a little harder.

As much as he knew he wanted her right now, he had to stay focused or else they could both end up dead. "Prissy, a lucky hair...thing? Come on."

"Ha!" She stood with a wide smile on her face and twirled a neon pink hair elastic around her finger. "Every year I've worn this, I've kicked ass. I'm not about to go without it now."

In a matter of seconds, Zack watched as she twisted her beautiful black hair into a ponytail. With her hair pulled back from her face, she looked more severe, but that sparkle of mischief was still in her eyes. *Spells*, she was the most beautiful woman he'd ever known.

Priscilla placed her hands on her hips and thrust her breasts out. "Now I'm ready to catch the bad guy and kick some ass."

His cock wanted some ass, but at that moment it certainly wasn't Josh's. Not wanting to distract her from their assignment, he went through a mental list of things guaranteed to make him soft. Nothing worked, so instead he turned and made his way out of the back room of Colard Castle and headed toward where the Cauldron Cup

144

Sweet and Spicy Spells

competition would be happening. Priscilla silently fell into step beside him.

"You'll be the bait in our little trap. Josh will be more likely to go for you than me."

"Why's that? He thinks he can take on a girl?" she snorted.

"Not at all. But he *knows* he can't take me on. Plus he saw the two of us together. He'll use our relationship to his advantage. Try to hurt you to get to me."

Priscilla stopped suddenly. "And would that work?"

Zack slowed down and stopped a few feet ahead of her. There was no way he'd turn around to face her. It would give too much away and he didn't want to do this now. They both needed their focus so they could get out of this in one piece. A quick glance at Priscilla though, and he knew he couldn't brush her off. Didn't want to do anything that would hurt her again. But if she really knew, if Josh found out how much she meant to him, they'd both be in trouble.

"Of course it would work. I wouldn't jeopardize anyone's life while trying to catch a crook. Josh is a bastard too and doesn't care."

He ignored the pain from the zap she shot into his ass.

"Does it matter, Zack?"

It went against every fiber of his being to do this, to tell her what she needed to hear. But he didn't want to be responsible for that light in her eyes going out. Not again.

"Yes. It matters."

In a poof, she was in front of him. The frown on her face caused her forehead to scrunch together. He thought she looked adorable.

"Then I shouldn't be here. The last thing I want is to get in the way and screw this up for you."

Zack reached up and brushed the back of his hand down along her cheek. When she leaned in against the contact, he felt

145

Christine d'Abo & Renee Field

an unexpected wave of tenderness wash over him. He had to swallow past a sudden lump in his throat to get the words out.

"You're not going to screw this up. Any doubts I might have had were obliterated by your performance back at Harry's. You're a better partner than Josh ever was."

That was the thing that pissed him off more than anything. He'd been partners with Josh for the past three years. Zack had taken him under his wing and shown him the ropes of being a warden. They'd had a lot of fun and kicked a lot of ass in that time. It had almost felt like it did when his father was alive.

But not once did he suspect Josh of being dirty. He should have known.

Out of nowhere, Priscilla punched him on the shoulder. "Stop that."

"Holy shit! What was that for?"

"I can feel and hear some of your thoughts now, remember? Stop blaming yourself. You heard the council. They trusted him too. They hadn't seen anything that would have led them to believe Josh was planning something like this. It's not your fault. Now stop it."

"Yes, ma'am," he said and smiled at her as he rubbed the tender spot on his shoulder. "So, are you ready for this?"

"Let's kick his ass," she winked. With a snap of her fingers, she poofed from sight.

Zack shook his head as he pulled his father's medallion from his coat pocket. Silently he slipped it over his head and tucked it safely under his shirt. The cool metal came to rest just above his heart and gave him a sense of peace.

"Time to kick ass indeed."

* * * * *

Priscilla squatted in the middle of the large ring that had been prepared for the Cauldron Cup and picked up a handful

146

Sweet and Spicy Spells

of the sand that had been laid. The playing field was more crowded than it had been in the past, the obstacles larger and more dangerous. It seemed that by kicking everyone's ass so badly for the past five years in a row, the wizards wanted to up the stakes. Large granite stones and tall silver obelisks were strategically positioned around the ring so it would be easy for the wizards doing battle to draw energy from them if needed.

The sand-covered floor would be her biggest advantage, but likely the only one she would have this year. She'd have to suggest that, when it was the witches' turn to host the Cup next year, they'd give the wizards pebbles.

Itty bitty pebbles.

"Well, well, well. Look who they let out of jail. Someone on the council must have bet a pretty penny on you winning again this year."

Priscilla stood and turned to face Josh. He was leaning against the largest of the granite boulders, arms crossed across his chest and an arrogant smirk on his face. If they'd met under different circumstances, she would have been attracted to him. There was something about the way he held his body, the tilt of his head that was familiar.

Too bad he was trying to get her killed.

"Hi, Josh. Well, it seems there wasn't enough evidence to hold me. Especially after they caught Jack from Harry's casting a naughty spell. You'd think even a nimrod like him would know you can't cast black magic in public. Oh well."

She made sure her tone was its usually snotty self, and even added an eye roll for good measure. And, as if on cue, she turned her back and marched to the middle of the ring.

"Now, if you don't mind, I only have ten minutes left to get a feel for the ring before the next contestant comes in for their prep time. You wouldn't want me to claim the wizards used unfair methods to throw me off."

"Yes, I heard your sister had a sudden and amazing display of spellcrafting back at Harry's. Who knew that a

147

Christine d'Abo & Renee Field

witch who couldn't conjure up a towel for her bath could create a time bubble? Seems a little out of her league, don'tcha think?"

How the fuck did he know about Kisha's towel? Her entire body tensed at the implication. He'd been watching her conversation with Kisha a few days ago. Before Zack and Foster had become tangled up in their lives. Why?

"Yes, she's been working extra hard this week. She might even kick my ass this year in the ring if she were competing." And if he even thought of going near Kisha, she'd tear him apart.

"It would be a shame to bruise such a lovely ass," he said in a less than flattering tone. "I'm surprised you're not with her now, Priscilla. She's taking her witches test, if I'm not mistaken."

Priscilla never thought anything sounded worse than when people called her Prissy. But the way Josh said her name made her skin crawl.

"She actually asked me not to be there. Said I was making her nervous. You know how little sisters can be," she said and shrugged.

"No. I have no idea."

Those simple words coming from him held more menace than any black magic he could have cast.

Nervous energy was pulsing through her. She needed every bit of it to brace herself for what was about to happen. The jolt was almost as good as the sexual charge Zack had given her earlier today, but nowhere near as satisfying. She'd have to get him to give her a repeat performance after this little diversion was over. And after winning the Cup.

Distracted by her own thoughts, she was surprised when Josh suddenly appeared in front of her. She recovered quickly and took a half step back, giving herself some much needed maneuvering room. Still holding the dirt from the ground in

Sweet and Spicy Spells

her hand, she moved it behind her slightly so he wouldn't see it.

"So, to answer your earlier question, yes, I do mind," he sneered at her. "I mind everything that this fucking impotent council has allowed to happen."

"Back off, Sparky." Priscilla took another step back as he pressed forward. "If you have a problem with the council, then take it up with them. I really don't give a rat's ass."

Priscilla felt the hair on her bare arms stand up, a telltale sign he was pulling energy from the environment around him. Knowing she was going to have to let him knock her around a little went against everything she believed in. Fucking pissed her off to be honest. But some things were more important than ego.

Winning, for instance.

"Gee, I never considered that, Prissy. What an excellent idea. I think I'll let the council know exactly what I think of them."

The sudden blast of energy caught her completely off guard. Priscilla flew through the air and landed in a heap on the ground ten feet away. She hadn't heard him cast the spell, but then again, if he was adept at using black magic, chances are he hadn't said very much. Most of those spells were silent and deadly. And he clearly wasn't as stupid as Jack.

This wasn't going to go well. She'd probably have to change her outfit before the competition, maybe even have to fix her hair. As long as he didn't kill her before Zack got his ass in gear to come help, she didn't really care.

Managing to hold onto the sand, she used it to cast a quick protection spell around her. At the very least, she'd save getting a few bruises.

She gave her head a hard shake, exaggerating the effects of the blast. He didn't know her at all if he thought that was enough to take her out. Oh well, it wouldn't be the first time in her life she'd had to put a man in his place.

149

Christine d'Abo & Renee Field

"What the fuck are you doing?" she yelled at him and jumped to her feet.

"Well, you see, your boyfriend is probably onto me by now. Zack may be a pompous ass, but he's not stupid."

"And he's *not* my boyfriend," she ground out between her teeth. That's the last thing she needed him to focus on right now. The closer he realized she and Zack were, the more likely he'd try to kill her. Or worse.

"I need to buy myself some insurance if he's going to cooperate with me. And that's you, sweetheart."

Before she had time to react, the ground beneath her began to rumble. She wasn't able to move as the ground seemed to reach up and bind her feet to it. The doors that led to the main part of Colard Castle slammed shut, blocking off a physical means of escape. She could only imagine what kind of spell he'd cast to stop others from coming in. When she tried to speak to cast a spell, she found her voice was gone. *Shit*! He was using a twisted version of her earth magic. Panic began to claw at her as her hands flew to her throat.

"I believe you pulled that little stunt on Jack back at the bar. Oh, don't look so surprised. Your little sister might look hot, but her skills are more than a little weak."

She swallowed hard but couldn't release the pressure on her throat. If he increased it at all, there'd be permanent damage. The only thing that was keeping her larynx from being crushed was her rapidly weakening protection spell.

"Now we're going to go on a little trip, and once we get there, I'll send your *boyfriend* a message. Or is he just your lover? Either way, he'll be so busy trying to find you, I'll be free to do what I need to."

"And what is that exactly, Josh?"

Priscilla felt relief as the pressure on her voice box disappeared when Josh turned to face Zack. A series of harsh coughs exploded from her as she gasped for air.

"Nice timing," she managed to croak out.

150

Sweet and Spicy Spells

Zack ignored her and kept his attention focused on Josh. With the two wizards intent on killing each other, it gave Priscilla an opportunity to shake off the effects of the spell and get back into the game.

"Yes, you always did seem to have nice timing, Zack. The council would remind us of that constantly." As Josh spoke, he moved away from Priscilla to circle around Zack. His back wasn't to her, but she wasn't in his direct line of sight anymore. That gave her a bit of an advantage.

"It wasn't a pissing match. We were partners. Fighting the bad guys together. Remember?" Zack kept his voice low, his eyes fixed on Josh.

Priscilla went through every mental exercise she could think of to steady her nerves. She needed to find the same place she'd managed to pull herself to back at Harry's. She needed to ground herself.

Of course!

The sand still held her feet in a vise-like grip, keeping her bound. But with the use of her voice, she didn't need to worry about that anymore. Josh had essentially turned her into an automatic weapon with unlimited ammunition, the earth feeding her power. She kept her chanting low so that Josh wouldn't realize what she was about to do.

Not that he would have cared at the moment. Josh growled as he launched an attack against Zack. A large bolt of electricity shot from the air above and almost landed fully on Zack. He'd managed to twist and raise a shield spell in time to deflect the bulk of the blast. Priscilla tried to ignore the hum from the granite stones around her as Zack took power to launch a counterattack of his own.

While the two wizards blasted spell after spell at each other, dodging and popping around the ring, Priscilla felt the air around her grow heavy. In her mind, she was able to see everything, feel the rhythm of life around her as it pulsed and flowed. Silently, she drew her energy from the ground, became connected with it and everything around her. She felt an overwhelming rush of power.

"*Tardesco*," she whispered.

Unlike at Harry's, time didn't stop. The area she had to control was just too large for her to hold time completely. Zack and Josh continued their forward motion, but it was so greatly reduced it almost looked comical. Broken free from the power of Josh's black magic, Priscilla was able to step clear of the sand prison around her feet.

It took her a second, but she realized Zack was in trouble. Walking up to him, she could see the look of determination and realization written over his face. Josh had somehow managed to send a paralyzing blast toward Zack at the same time he caused the sand to reach up and capture his foot in much the same way he'd trapped her. With a snap of her fingers, the sand receded and Zack began to twist to the side unimpeded. But it still wasn't enough. Josh was stronger than either of them individually because of his use of the black magic. If they were able to join forces, they could beat him.

Stepping behind Zack, Priscilla slipped her arms under his and pulled him a safe distance from the blast. Despite the danger, she couldn't stop the shiver of awareness she felt whenever they'd gotten close. But more than that, she realized she needed him more than just in her bed. And they both damn well better survive this mess so she could tell him that. She straightened his body up to a stand and laced his fingers through hers.

"Zack, just go with me on this one," she whispered against his ear.

With a snap of her fingers, time returned to its normal speed. The paralyzing blast hit empty ground, sending a cloud of dust and dirt flying into the air. It was all the cover they needed. Priscilla poofed them behind the large granite boulder and she yanked Zack down to a squat.

Sweet and Spicy Spells

"Nice timing, sweetheart," he said and winked at her. "Now what?"

"Don't know about you, but I'm getting bored with this shit. Time for a little bag and grab."

Zack's smile spread at the sound of Josh's pissed off wail. "You bag, I'll grab."

They instantly poofed back to where Josh stood, one on each side of him. He was panting hard, his face was pale and his hands were shaking.

"I think we've all had enough," Zack said in a low, steady voice. "If you turn yourself in, the council may be convinced to be lenient. Only give you life in prison."

"And let you ride off into the sunset? Fuck you, Zack."

Priscilla watched Zack tense, but she didn't jump in. She knew him well enough to know he had to try one more time to save his former friend.

"You're weak. Tired. Let me take you in. Make this easier for you."

"I'm stronger than I've ever been. You have no idea the power I can wield, what these dark spells can do, Zack. Neither did your father."

Priscilla watched the blood drain from Zack's face. *Oh no. No, no, no, not this.*

"What?" Zack whispered.

"Oh, he thought he could beat me too, but he was so weak. It took nothing for me to rip him apart."

"You bastard!" Zack yelled and threw a large fireball at Josh.

"Zack, no!"

Zack, sweetie, listen to me. You can't do this alone. Nothing— Zach was ignoring her.

Priscilla poofed to the side of the boulder to keep from getting hit by the wild lightning bolts Josh and Zack were

153

throwing at each other. Her heart almost broke with the look of pain on Zack's face.

"I used to laugh at you, Zack. Every time you whined about your daddy," Josh taunted him. "You and your little piss-ant brother."

Zack let out a yell and dove at Josh. The two of them rolled on the ground, Zack throwing several punches at Josh, bloodying his face.

"Zack, stop!"

"Priscilla, back off," Zack warned, taking another swing. Josh took advantage of the momentary distraction to blink away.

Priscilla could feel Zack's pain through their link. She remembered it, had lived through it herself with the deaths of her own parents. No, she'd had enough of this shit. She took a breath and blinked a few feet to the left of Josh.

"You're under arrest, asshole," she ground out.

"Fuck you," Josh spat at her. "I'm going to tear you apart once I'm through with him."

"Okay, this warden stuff is lame." Priscilla rolled her eyes. "*Caeco!*"

Josh's eyes flew open wide a second before his hands covered them.

"You bitch! I can't see!"

"*Obrigesco.*" Zack's voice came from beside her.

Josh stood completely still. They'd managed to stop him for the time being. Priscilla sauntered over to where he stood, patted his cheek and clicked a magical set of handcuffs around his wrists. "Now the council can deal with your murdering ass."

With a snap of her fingers, Josh disappeared from sight, but she swore she heard him scream as he went. No, the council wouldn't be very kind with their punishment.

"Well," she said and smiled. "I guess that's everything."

Sweet and Spicy Spells

Zack was standing there, silently staring at the place where Josh just was. His thoughts were racing so much Priscilla couldn't keep up with them. He needed time and space to work through everything and she doubted they had much of either.

She gave him a few moments alone before she approached. She knew he blamed himself for not seeing through Josh's disguise sooner. She sighed and made her way over to him. Taking his hand in hers, she gave it a squeeze.

"You okay?"

The smile he gave her didn't quite reach his eyes. "No."

She knew exactly how he felt. "You will be," she said quietly.

He arched a single eyebrow but didn't say anything in response. Priscilla didn't know if this was the right time or not, but she'd been putting it off. If they really were going to try to make this thing between them work, everything had to be out in the air.

"When you left five years ago, do you remember what we were supposed to do?"

His steady stare told her all she needed to know.

"A date, Zack. You'd promised to take me somewhere special to make up for bailing on a previous date. Dinner, dancing and a promise that I could do whatever I wanted to you. Instead you told me you were going away and we were through."

The memory, once painful, now filled her with a dull ache. Even after all these years. Zack nodded and brought her hand up to his lips. His touch was so soft, gentle, she knew it was his way of saying sorry. A tingle of electricity surged between them at the contact, making Priscilla gasp.

"I remember. I wanted to save you the pain of being with me. You wouldn't know where I was or what I'd be doing. At the time, I didn't think you could handle it."

155

"I probably couldn't." The words hurt to say, but she wasn't about to start lying to herself now. "You walking out of my life the way you did, in a strange way, was good for me. I'm a stronger person today."

"And one fucking unbelievable witch. How the hell do you slow time like that?"

With a gentle tug, he pulled her hard against him. The scent of his body sent hers racing into overdrive again. His skin was hot, sweaty from the fight with Josh, his muscles tight under her touch. Her pussy was wet from wanting, needing him.

"*Spells*, you're hot, Cilly," he murmured against her hair.

"You're just saying that because you're scared I'm going to kick your ass at the Cup."

She gave him a wicked grin as she reached down and grabbed his growing erection through his pants. "See, I make a much more enjoyable partner than Josh."

Someone cleared their throat behind them. One of the council members stood behind them, his black hood pushed off his head to reveal a weathered face and rich brown eyes.

"That is an interesting proposition, Ms. Morgan."

Priscilla started to pull away from Zack, but he held her tight against him. Instead of the fear most magic users had for the nameless council members, he didn't seem affected.

"Did you have enough proof against Josh to clear us?" Zack asked in a calm voice.

"Yes. It didn't take long for him to make...a full confession."

Priscilla shuddered as a slow grin spread across the council member's face.

"I'll need you both to return to the council chambers. There is another matter that needs resolution before you can participate in the competition."

"We'll return momentarily," Zack nodded.

Sweet and Spicy Spells

"Wait," Priscilla jumped in. "Kisha? Did she pass her test?"

The elder smiled. "I wasn't going anywhere. But yes, she did pass, which is one of the reasons you must return as soon as possible."

Priscilla grinned. "Oh thank the *spells*! I'm so happy for her."

"See, I told you Foster was the right wizard for the job."

"Shut up. Let's go now, Zack." She slipped her arm in his and gave it a squeeze.

The elder coughed lightly, drawing Priscilla's attention back to him.

"Before you leave, I'd like to discuss another matter with you. Ms. Morgan?"

"Yes?" Her heart was pounding in her chest, but the fact Zack was beside her, offering her support, made her feel safe.

"The council has been watching you for some time now."

Shit. "Look, I know I'm not the nicest witch out there. Okay, I can be a complete arrogant bitch at times. But I've never crossed the line."

The council member nodded. "Of course. That's why I'm here. How would you like a job?"

157

Chapter Twelve

Foster couldn't believe what his eyes and ears had seen or heard. He felt as if he'd been punched in the gut repeatedly. And that was exactly what he planned to do to one Josh Neil. Then he'd kill the bastard, slowly. The evil rage left him seeing spots. He'd never experienced fury like that before. He still couldn't believe what he'd learned.

Josh Neil, his friend forever, had murdered their father. Josh Neil was the one trying to take over the council through the use of black magic. Josh Neil was his father's bastard son. That one seemed to hurt most of all. And he was at a loss to explain that feeling, because he ached for retribution.

So when someone had fired a deadly blast aiming for Kisha's head, Foster didn't think twice. He used his magic to form a shield around Kisha — anything to keep her safe. Now Foster planned on using that blast as an excuse to go after Josh, who had dared to try to harm the witch of his life before being forcibly placed in the punishment chair. Only problem was his brother got to him before he did.

"No one ever saw it coming," said Josh, straining against the magical bonds, which now made it impossible for him to move or use magic.

Josh had been brought in by Zack and Priscilla and he seemed to delight in telling all the council elders just how stupid they all had been to trust him so easily.

"Why?"

The question was asked by Zack, who had zapped back inside the council room with Priscilla.

Sweet and Spicy Spells

A part of Foster couldn't believe his brother was asking the man who had murdered their father why, while another part wanted to know.

"You Kane men are all the same. When my mother informed me what she did to conceive me and when I confronted Magnus with what I had learned, you know what that man said to me? He said, 'Josh, it was a mistake.'"

Foster watched as Josh visibly shook.

"I am not a mistake. He wouldn't recognize me. You have no idea how that made me feel. I could only watch the two of you. A part of the family as a friend, but none of it was real. How would you feel?"

There was a part of Foster that, while still fuming over what he'd learned, also sympathized with how Josh must have felt. *Still, that doesn't excuse his actions.*

"That doesn't excuse your actions. That doesn't excuse the use of black magic," said Zack in his even voice, echoing Foster's thoughts.

"Shut up, Zack. I'm going to kill him," said Foster, attempting to move forward. He felt Kisha's small hand come to rest on his arm. He hadn't even realized she'd broken free from the protective shield he'd cast. Her touch stilled him, calmed the angry thoughts that were flying through his mind.

"No, you aren't." Zack stood directly in front of Foster.

Foster didn't hesitate. He pushed aside his brother, only to be thrown back onto his ass. "Get out of my way, bro," he growled, quickly standing.

"He's our *brother*," said Zack.

Like that makes any sense. "So what? He murdered our father!"

"No, I don't think he did," said Kisha.

"There's only one way to find out," said Priscilla.

"Wait, before you do that, we need to time-freeze Josh," said Zack, moving to face the council elders.

"That sounds like a plan. The last thing I want is for him to attempt anything on my sister again," echoed Priscilla, lacing her fingers automatically through Zack's.

A firm nod from the Council Head assured them they could proceed.

Priscilla time-froze Josh while Foster reached for that special channel he'd developed with Kisha.

"Sweetlips, tell me it's going to be okay," said Foster.

Kisha nodded.

A second later, the four of them were zapped from the council room.

Foster heard Kisha hiccup on a sob.

"I'm really beginning to hate this place," said Kisha.

Foster watched Kisha wrinkle her nose as the rank odor of the prison assaulted their sense of smell.

"This place smells worse every time I come back," said Priscilla.

"There's nothing in this cell. Why are we here, Kisha?" asked Zack, ever the practical one.

Foster watched as Kisha knelt down and placed her hands palm down on the cold compact cell floor. He knew exactly what she was doing. *The question is why? Why is she calling the rats to her again?* Foster fought the urge to shiver. He hated rats. "Kisha, sweetlips, what are you doing?"

"I'm trying to see if this will work. I'm not sure if he's still alive, but I've got to try," said Kisha, closing her eyes so she could focus on the task.

"Is she doing what I think she's doing?" asked Zack.

"Sadly, yup. She's calling the rats to her again. The bigger question is why?" answered Priscilla.

Another second, all four of them heard what sounded like a dozen rats scurry to their position. Through a small hole in the right hand corner of the cell, they watched as the rats squeezed their bodies through. One large and particularly ugly

Sweet and Spicy Spells

rat had a difficult time getting its body through the small opening. Once through, it pushed its way to the front and then raised itself up on its hind legs to look at Kisha.

"He seems to know you, Kisha," said Foster.

"I'm hoping," Kisha replied.

"Shut up, Zack. Leave my sister alone. Take your time, Kis. I just *love* spending time in this dungeon," said Priscilla sarcastically.

"All of you can it. I trust you, Kisha," said Foster.

Kisha nodded. "Is that you, Magnus?"

"Magnus? As in my father? Kisha, it's a rat, not my father," said Foster.

Foster watched his brother kneel down beside the large rat.

"Is it him?" Zack asked, directing his question to Kisha.

"I think it is. It's hard to tell. It's been five years and he's learned to adapt so much that I'm finding it hard to pick up any traces of magic," replied Kisha.

Zack stood up, turning to face Foster. "If we link as brothers, we should be able to find a magical link if it's our father."

"You can't be serious. Father is dead," replied Foster.

"Kisha, can you tell me what makes you think this rat is Magnus?"

Kisha squatted down next to the rat and held her hand out as an offering. Foster watched the large rat timidly approach. The rat sniffed her hand and then buried its ugly, scarred face into her palm.

"I'm positive. It's him. As part of my final test, the council zapped me back in time and I believe it was with a purpose in mind. They transformed me into a rat and I heard a man being tortured. It was Magnus. Josh was beating him. I knew I didn't have much time and the only spell I could think of to work was the life for a life spell. I summoned a rat to the cell and exchanged their lives. The rat became the man whom everyone assumed was your father and your father is this rat," said Kisha with conviction.

"My father is this rat?" said Foster, moving forward to study the rat in question.

Foster watched as Priscilla approached her sister. "Kisha, only you can change him back. But first I think Zack and Foster need to link and attempt to seek out the magical link with their father."

"You're right, Priscilla," agreed Zack. "On the count of three, Foster. One. Two. Three."

Foster closed his eyes, letting the inherent familiar magical link he had with his brother reach out and touch Zack. Goose bumps formed on his skin as the magic within him doubled. Then he felt Zack's magic twin with his to reach out to the rat. And there, in a small portion of the rat, Foster felt it. He felt the knowing. Felt the family magic and knew — this rat was his father. His heart felt heavy with the knowing, with the relief he felt at having his father back.

"It's him," said Foster. "It's our father."

"Change him back, Kisha," said Zack.

Foster heard Kisha's words.

"*Averto!*" The word flashed through the walls of the small cell, echoing loudly through the dungeon.

Then everyone blinked as Magnus Kane transformed into his original wizard self.

"Thank you," said Magnus, reaching out to hug Kisha, who was nearest to him.

Foster watched Kisha accept his father's powerful bear hug. She smiled with relief. He knew exactly how she felt.

"Good to know you found one who can cook, Foster," said his father, winking at him.

Sweet and Spicy Spells

Foster blinked. "Dad? Is it really you? I can't believe it. For five years I've been hunting for the person who killed you and all this time you were alive."

Foster watched his father pull away from Kisha to make his way to him. Magnus was a head taller than Foster, but he had always been an affectionate man and he didn't hesitate to pull Foster into a huge bear hug.

"I am so sorry for what you two must have gone through. Please forgive me," said Magnus, hugging Foster tight.

Then Magnus released Foster, turning his attention once again to Kisha. "The final test the council elders gave you was a surprise to me. But I must say you even surprised them, Kisha. I told you to tell my boys I loved them, and while you said yes, it wasn't enough for you. You were able to perform one of the most complicated spells without thought. You are a true Morgan Witch. And I would be honored to have you as a daughter-in-law, witch."

"Father!" shouted Foster, not quite believing what his father had just said. "This is not the time for that. I'm still having a hard enough time with the fact that you were a rat and are alive."

"Alive all thanks to that witch of yours, Foster. Son, I know this has been especially hard on you and your brother. Let me assure you I plan to make it up to both of you," declared Magnus.

Magnus then walked over to embrace Zack.

"You have a lot of explaining to do, Father," said Zack.

"Good to know you have fulfilled your duty, son," said Magnus, ruffling Zack's hair like he was a child

"And you, my dear, are the challenge my Zack needs. I know my two boys will do the right thing. Now, before we leave, I must ask. What did you do with Josh?"

"Josh? You mean your bastard son?" Foster couldn't help the sarcastic tone in his voice.

163

Christine d'Abo & Renee Field

"I will explain all of that in time, but for now, you two must trust me."

Foster backed up. "Trust you? I thought you were dead. I thought Josh was my friend. None of this makes sense."

Kisha placed her hand in Foster's and gave it a gentle squeeze. "You're always telling me to trust you. I think the time has come for you to trust your father."

Foster didn't know what to think. He wanted answers. *Now! Not later. Now!* "Fine."

A moment later, all five of them were zapped back before the council elders.

Another round of applause greeted them.

"You, Kisha Morgan, have passed the council's test. You are a full-fledged witch with honors."

"With honors," gasped Priscilla and Kisha.

"With honors. The red magic runs deep within you, but you use it only for good, and for that we have granted you the distinction of Witch with Honors," said the Council Head.

"As for you, Josh Neil."

The Council Head unzapped Josh from the time-freeze Zack and Priscilla had leveled at him.

"Wait, I'd like a chance to speak," asked Magnus, addressing the council.

"As you wish," said the Council Head.

"Josh, can you ever forgive me?" asked Magnus.

"Forgive you? He tried to kill you," shouted Foster, stunned with his father's declaration.

"Hear me out, Foster. When I found out Josh was really my son, I didn't do the right thing by him. I was furious at him, but the treachery wasn't his. It was his mother's. His mother tricked me into meeting with her, with me believing it was a secret special rendezvous with my wife. She then used a spell to take on your mother's appearance and voice to get what she wanted — a child.

164

Sweet and Spicy Spells

"You, Josh, like me, were used by your mother. She wanted a link to the Kane fortune and Kane magic and knew the only way to get that was to trick me into believing I was with my wife, whom I have loved since the first time I met her. When Josh told me what had happened, I was stunned. When he provided proof from his mother, I should never have turned him away. It wasn't your fault, Josh. For that I ask your forgiveness. I wasn't man enough to tell my wife what had happened, even though I knew she would have believed me, would have kept on loving me always."

"Father, she never stopped loving you. But when she found out you were dead, it was like her life stopped. She just couldn't go on without you," declared Zack.

"I know. Even though I was transformed into a rat, the magical link we had enabled me to feel her as much as possible. I felt the exact moment when her life ended. My only regret is that I played a part in that. She loved me too much to let go."

"It wasn't your fault, Father. It was his!" said Foster, pointing at Josh.

"Maybe, but Josh too has been a pawn in this game. Even so, I should never have hurt you. You are my son, Josh," said Magnus, turning to look at Josh.

"With the council's permission, I ask that they reverse history so that I may make things right," said Magnus, stunning everyone.

"What will you give us in return for this favor?" asked the Council Head.

"I will pledge to return to the council for eternity," declared Magnus, bowing his head.

"It is as you request. Thank you, Magnus. The council is in need of your skills."

"It is I who should thank you. I am sorry, Josh, that I was not wizard enough to acknowledge you when you came forward. For that I will ask your forgiveness every day. But with the council's privilege, we are rewriting history. Yes, none of what has happened will take place."

"Wait a sec," said both Foster and Zack.

"We want to remember," they said again in unison.

Magnus chuckled. "Boys, you will remember all you need to remember, but the rest will be rewritten. Make it so!"

Sweet and Spicy Spells

Chapter Thirteen

᎒

Priscilla stepped into the middle of the ring for the fifth time that night. A bead of sweat had dripped down behind her corset and was making the side of her breasts itchy. She was tired, but totally psyched at the same time.

This was it.

The crowd started to chant like crazy when Zack walked onto the field to stand across from her. They'd both had to face some of the toughest witches and wizards to get to this point. It had come close a few times tonight. She couldn't keep her stupid mind focused on what was going on half the time. And now that she was about to face Zack, she needed total control.

Foster and Kisha had been screwing around all night. And because of their stupid link, it was getting harder and harder for her to concentrate on the fighting matches and not on the fact she was horny as hell.

If she were allowed to fuck Zack right now, she would.

The only comforting thing was the fact he'd been just as distracted as she'd been when he'd fought. There was once when she thought he was going to lose. A young wizard, just having passed his council test, almost got a lucky shot off. She actually found herself holding her breath when Zack had to bend his body at an awkward angle to avoid the energy blast. He'd barely rolled to the right and gotten off his own shot in time. A half second later and she would be fighting a kid right now.

Damn good thing he'd won. Now none of the other battles mattered. It was just him and her facing off to prove once and for all that she was the best.

167

Christine d'Abo & Renee Field

"Oh, I don't think so, *Prissy*," Zack waggled his finger at her. "You're going down this fight."

I hate it when you call me that and you know it!

Why do you think I use it?

Get out of my head! I hate that too, Kane.

I'd rather be in your pants.

Bah!

The wizards in the crowd went crazy, cheering echoing in the arena. The witches were just as loud, booing Zack and shouting out their support for her. She cracked her knuckles and moved her head from side to side to loosen up the muscles. She felt the current of energy running between them. The sensual pull that tweaked her senses, heightened her awareness of everything around her. Including Zack.

"How are your *spells* holding up? Getting tired from seeing all this action? I'll let you have a little break if you want to rest up," she said with a saucy smile.

"Don't you worry about my *spells*. I've saved my big ones for the last."

He'd shed his normal dress shirt and put on a form-fitting t-shirt. It clung so tightly to his body she swore she could count every one of his abs through the material. She could feel the energy in the arena change every time he walked onto the floor. Every witch in the room wanted to fuck him senseless. She knew the second this match was done, win or lose, he'd have to fight them off with a broom.

They'd have to get past her first. And she wasn't about to let anyone get near him. Somewhere in the back of her mind she heard Zack chuckle.

"Contestants, this is the final match," the loud voice of the referee boomed. The tall skinny man was dressed all in black and floated above the arena so he'd be able to quickly spot a hit. The crowd went nuts while Priscilla and Zack stood there, grinning.

Sweet and Spicy Spells

"Please listen while we review the rules," the referee continued. "You must stay within the field of play. There is to be no pulling objects from outside of the arena. Use only what is before you. This match will be played as a best of three. The first player to be cut twice loses."

The crowd began to taunt Zack, herself and the other audience members. The energy they created was almost overpowering. But she knew she'd be able to use it to her advantage.

"Contestants, are you ready?" the referee said even louder than before, stirring up the already insane crowd.

"Yes," Zack said seriously and let the grin drop from his face.

"Let's do this," she said, matching his tone.

"Please take your positions."

Both she and Zack walked to their assigned spots and waited for the referee to signal the start of the match. The crowd instantly silenced and Priscilla took a deep breath to relax her body and clear her mind.

She was so going to kick ass.

Don't count on it, Prissy.

"Begin!"

Neither one of them moved. The crowd was on its feet screaming and cheering, demanding that they take some sort of action. But Priscilla simply waited, raising a single eyebrow in question. Zack answered with an eyebrow raise of his own.

We best give them what they want, Prissy.

She was able to dodge out of the way of the lightning blast easily. The wizards roared, encouraging Zack.

"Missed me," she winked.

"Playing with you," he grinned.

Priscilla gave him a mental shove and poofed herself on top of one of the granite boulders behind him. She could have zapped his ass with a shock of her own but didn't.

You're quick, Cilly.

I can go all night long, baby.

Tease.

Zack poofed himself over to an opposite boulder closer to the witches' side of the arena.

"Baby, see me after—"

"I'll screw your brains out—"

"Show us your ass—"

One of the witches went so far as to zap Zack's shirt away. The wizard crowd began to protest as the witches were screaming out their approval.

The referee held up his hand to pause the match. "If this crowd doesn't behave, I will remove you all!"

A chorus of boos and applause circled the arena. Priscilla couldn't help but notice Zack didn't put a new shirt on. She mentally kicked herself when she caught herself staring at his perfectly formed pecs and the dark sprinkling of hair that covered his chest. He flexed his arms and the witches cheered. For half a second, she thought he was playing up to the crowd.

There's only one witch I'm interested in. I want to give you something nice to look at. Call it your second place prize.

You're such a pig, Zack.

She hoped he didn't pick up on the fact that her pussy was dripping wet just from looking at him.

She'd had enough of this. "Time to say goodbye."

Priscilla jumped off the boulder at the same time as she sent a blast of cold air at him. The wind picked up bits of sand from the floor and Zack had to close his eyes to protect them before he could raise a protection shield. That gave her the opening she needed. She sent a sharp bolt that hit him on the side of his arm, causing a light cut.

"First blood, Priscilla Morgan!"

Sweet and Spicy Spells

The witches went wild. Priscilla couldn't take her eyes off the small red line that now graced the most perfect biceps she'd ever seen. The man had no right to be that hot.

Zack's gaze went from his arm to Priscilla and back again.

"You cut me," he said, sounding very much surprised.

"I believe those *are* the rules. Need a bandage?"

He narrowed his gaze, gave his hands a shake and dug his feet into the ground. "Time to get down to business."

She smiled and beckoned him with her finger.

This time she knew he meant business, could tell by the way he marched up to his mark. As soon as the referee yelled *begin!* Priscilla was forced to dodge and block an onslaught of electric jolts coming from Zack. She had to use every ounce of her concentration to be able to hold his attacks off while getting shots off of her own. She even tried to poof away to buy some breathing space, but Zack barely gave her a second to catch her breath. He was unrelenting in his attack and had her completely on the defensive.

When she tried to run across the arena floor, Priscilla suddenly found herself blinded. She didn't need her eyes to know where the boulders were, but she did need them to see his attacks. She almost made it to the nearest boulder when she felt the bite of his attack zap her ass.

"First blood, Zack Kane!"

She gave her head a shake and the blinding spell cleared.

"That was a lucky shot," she said, walking back to their marks, dusting the sand off her pants.

"Oh, I was aiming for your ass. No luck there."

Suddenly she felt invisible fingers caress the spot around where he'd cut her.

It's such a shame to hurt such a wonderful bottom.

You can kiss it when we're done here.

I'm going to do more than kiss your ass.

Christine d'Abo & Renee Field

She was about to send another teasing retort when she felt a powerful wave of desire wash through her. Her nipples instantly puckered in her corset and her pussy pulsed. The sensation was so powerful, it almost knocked her off her feet.

"What the fuck?" she whispered.

"Shit," Zack said at the same time.

They looked at each other and realized immediately what was happening. Kisha and Foster—they were fucking again!

"Great," she sighed.

"Contestants, you have each drawn first blood," the referee announced. "We are at sudden death. The next cut wins the Cauldron Cup!"

The crowd began its riot of cheers and whistles again, but Priscilla was barely aware of them. The mental connection she and Zack had formed with Kisha and Foster hadn't been severed. Now they were being bombarded with the side effects of hot sex.

Shooting Zack a quick look, she could see the growing bulge of his crotch and the pained expression on his face. Neither one of them were going to be in any shape for this next round.

"Oh, this should be fun," she muttered.

"Are you ready?" the referee shouted. They both nodded. "Begin!"

Instead of jumping to attack each other, they began walking a slow circle around the center of the arena. Closer and closer they moved in until they were only a few feet away. Priscilla sucked in a breath when she felt invisible fingers caress her painfully taut nipples.

"Shit, Zack," she groaned.

"Wasn't me," he said through his clenched teeth.

"Well then, your brother knows how to turn a woman on." She couldn't stop the sigh that escaped her when she felt her pussy tingle.

Sweet and Spicy Spells

Zack dove at her and they fell together to the ground in a heap. She managed to use his momentum to roll him onto his back and pin his arms back with her hands. Straddling his waist, she could feel his hard cock straining to be freed. She wanted to pull it out right then and there and run her tongue along the length of his hard shaft.

"If you keep thinking those thoughts, I'm going to embarrass myself."

"I wouldn't want you to do that," she smiled down at him.

In a blink he rolled her over so she was on her back. Besides sending another cheer through the crowd, it had the added bonus of letting him grind his cock against her pussy. She groaned again.

"You like that, baby? Want some more?"

She looked into his eyes and saw the intense desire looking back down at her. *Oh yeah, do I want more.* She wanted everything that was Zack Kane.

"We can't get out of here until a winner is declared," she said and made a lame attempt at struggling.

They both stopped their sparring and moaned when they felt a sudden rush of pleasure push through them. One or both of their siblings had just had an amazing orgasm.

"Fuck," Zack moaned.

"There's only one way we are going to get out of this," she said.

Another brief struggle found Priscilla back on top. Her hair was almost completely out of her hair elastic and fell to drape Zack's face.

"And what's that?" he asked, bucking his hips hard up against her.

She dipped her head down and bit his shoulder. Hard.

"Winner! Priscilla Morgan has drawn second blood!"

"Thank the spells." Zack rolled her over onto her back again.

The insanity of the crowd's cheers was suddenly silenced and Priscilla felt the hard sand beneath her change into the heavenly feel of satin sheets.

"You cheated." He nipped her neck.

"I never cheat. The rule was to draw blood. Didn't state how."

Zack rose to his knees above her and looked down at her like an aroused god. His neck was red from her lipstick and the bite she'd given his neck. His arm was also red from her earlier attack.

He was the sexiest man she'd ever seen.

"I think I'll punish you anyway," he said with a devilish grin.

In a blink, she found herself lying across Zack's lap on the bed wearing the silk skirt she'd worn earlier at Harry's. Slowly, he traced a line with his finger across her ass.

"I wonder how badly I cut your earlier. It was hard to tell with all the clothing you were wearing."

"Are you going to render first aid, Mr. Kane?"

"I'll do what I can to save such a lovely specimen."

His fingers were warm as he slid them under her skirt and pulled it up, revealing her naked skin to the cool bedroom air.

"How bad is it?" she said over her shoulder.

"You'll live to shake it another day." He traced a circle around the cut.

The gentleness of his touch made her relax. Which was why she let out a sharp cry when his hand connected squarely with her uninjured buttock, catching her unprepared.

"Zack!"

"I told you I was going to punish you."

Sweet and Spicy Spells

Her ass burned where his hand had connected, despite the fact he was already caressing it gently again.

"I just didn't think your punishment would be so swift."

He gave her ass another smack, which caused her to grind her hips down in an effort to escape. That motion rewarded her by drawing a groan from him as she pushed her wet pussy against his hard cock, which was still trapped in his pants.

The stinging of her ass turned into a burning tingle that made its way straight to her cunt. She wiggled her ass at him as she balled the sheets with her hands.

"What do you want, Prissy? Tell me," he cooed in her ear.

"Touch me," she moaned.

"Where?"

"Put your fingers in my pussy."

"Hmm, I'll have to think about it"

"Zack, please."

Priscilla bit her bottom lip when she felt him sit up and his fingers return to her ass. He let her part her legs slightly, giving his hand better access to her pussy and clit. Far slower than she would have liked, he began to dip his fingers into her cunt before teasing her from her clit to her asshole.

"Look at how wet you are. Do you like being spanked?"

"I'm a bad girl."

"How bad? Will you let me do this?"

With his finger wet from her cream, Zack pushed two fingers into her pussy while he pushed another into her ass. Priscilla moaned loudly as he worked his hand in both holes. When he used an invisible finger to stroke her clit, it was more than she could take.

"Fuck, I'm coming!" She moaned and bucked against him as her body clenched through the waves of pleasure. It was only when she collapsed that he slowed his motions.

Christine d'Abo & Renee Field

"Have I told you how unbelievably hot you are?" he said and caressed her ass again.

"Once or twice. But please, don't stop."

"I'm far from done with you."

Zack rolled her onto her back, and with a snap of his fingers, her clothing was gone. She stretched and rolled, her body still alive from her first orgasm. As his eyes traveled down the length of her, she felt the direction his thoughts were taking. Oh, she really liked where they were going.

"Like what you see?" she cooed.

"You're the hottest witch out there, baby. Hot and spicy."

"Hotter than the horde of horny women back at the arena? There were more than a few of them willing to take you home."

When his eyes met hers, Priscilla felt her heart do a flip. He looked at her with such love and possessiveness, she finally felt whole.

"There's only ever been you, Cilly."

Not willing to give into the tears that threatened to erupt from her, instead she opened her legs wide, wet her fingers with her mouth and reached down to play with her clit.

"Then get your ass over here and show me before I have fun all by myself."

With a primal growl, Zack threw himself on her. She wasn't sure whose magic was used to get rid of his clothing, and really who cared as long as he was sinfully naked.

He began to rub his cock against the side of her thigh, teasing her with his thrusts. But she wasn't about to let him get the upper hand again. This time it was her turn to cast, and in a blink, she had Zack's arms bound to the headboard with silk ropes.

"Aww, Cilly. You never did play fair."

176

Sweet and Spicy Spells

"I think you deserve a little punishment of your own. For making me wait five years before you fucked me. Longer even."

"Had I known how hot you were, I would have quit years ago and come running back to you."

Kneeling between his legs, she pulled her lucky hair elastic off the rest of the way and threw it to the floor.

"It might get lost," he said with a grin.

"I don't need it anymore."

With her hair free, she was able to spread the long strands over most of his stomach and groin. She knew her hair was soft and it would drive him mad. Letting it tease him for a moment, she enjoyed the feel of him tensing beneath her. When she didn't think he could take anymore, she rocked forward and licked up the length of his hard cock.

"*Spells*," he groaned.

"They have nothing to do with it." And she licked him again.

She dipped her head low enough to suck his left nut into her mouth, teasing his sac with her tongue. She felt the bed shake as he jerked his arms in an attempt to touch her.

"Fuck."

After a minute, she turned her attention to the other nut, licking small circles across his sac and teasing his shaft with her hand. Her thumb crested the head of his cock and felt a bead of pre-cum. Needing to taste him, she traced her tongue up his shaft to the head and proceeded to lick him clean.

"Yummy," she purred against him.

"There's more where that came from," he said and rocked his hips against her mouth.

Over and over, she swallowed him whole. Priscilla loved the feel of his cock as she pushed him deep into her throat, tasting his very essence. She licked and sucked him until she felt his body shake beneath her.

Christine d'Abo & Renee Field

"Baby, if you're going to ride me, best hop on. I can't hold on much longer."

She didn't need to be told twice. Priscilla pulled her body along the length of his, dragging her breasts across his stomach, stopping to lick his nipples before coming to snake her hands around his shoulders.

Without a word, she positioned her body above his cock and pushed herself down on him. Simultaneously, they moaned as he stretched her pussy with his girth. Sighs and moans passed between them as she began a steady rhythm, riding his shaft with slow precision.

It only took a minute for the tingle to return to her pussy and for her muscles to slowly milk his cock. She bit her lower lip and closed her eyes, concentrating on her approaching orgasm.

"That's it, baby. Ride me. Harder."

Priscilla ground her cunt hard against him, teasing her exposed clit with his pubic hair. She sucked in a breath when she suddenly felt his hands on her breasts, pulling her toward his mouth.

"Cheater," she whispered.

"Your fault. They're too perfect."

With one nipple in his mouth and the second rolled between his fingers, Priscilla knew she wouldn't last any longer. When Zack started sending her images of what he planned to do to her, it was all she needed to push her over the edge.

Zack covered her mouth in a searing kiss as she came, capturing her cries with his mouth. Their breath mingled as their minds came together. She knew he was close too. Looking at him, she could see the intense control he was holding over his body.

Look at me. I want to watch you come.

He groaned.

178

Sweet and Spicy Spells

Let go, Zack.

He opened his eyes and she could see it. He loved her. She felt it with every fiber of his body and hers.

Cilly.

Zack's body began to shake and he thrust madly into her. She tried to keep up with his frantic pace, but finally gave up and let her body relax into him. Zack sucked in a deep breath and his whole body stilled for a fraction of a second before he cried out and pounded hard and fast into her. Priscilla was caught off guard as she came with him, her third orgasm of the night.

Everything around them stilled. The noises of the night outside faded into nothing more than a low buzz. Priscilla vaguely registered the fact that Zack used a spell to pull the sheets up to cover them against the cool evening air.

"I love you," he whispered against the top of her head.

Priscilla's heart soared. She looked up into his eyes and smiled. All the past hurt was suddenly gone because she had her Zack back. And this time he was here to stay.

"I love you too," she sighed and snuggled in next to him.

"Promise me one thing, Cilly?"

"Hmm?"

"You'll protect me next time I go to Harry's. I think a lot of wizards are going to be pissed that I lost the Cup."

"Don't worry, baby. I'll protect you. If they call you a loser, I'll kick their ass for you."

Zack chuckled and rolled over to spoon her. The last thing Priscilla remembered before she drifted to sleep was Zack's rich baritone voice chuckling in her head.

I've definitely come out the winner. I have you.

* * * * *

179

Christine d'Abo & Renee Field

"Rats, I've added too many chocolate chips," said Kisha, trying to make the wooden spoon move the huge amount of cookie dough in the large ceramic bowl.

"There is no such thing as too many chocolate chips," admonished Foster, materializing next to the bowl of cookie dough.

"Don't even think it," said Kisha, smiling.

"Think what?"

"Foster Kane, I just know you're going to try to steal some of my cookie dough and I need all of it. I promised to make these for Priscilla. They're my wedding gift to her. There's a special ingredient in them."

Foster laughed. It was a deep-throated chuckle that filled the warm kitchen with happiness and left Kisha feeling tingly everywhere. Out of the corner of her eye, she spied him whisking his hand in the bowl, lightning fast, to steal a handful of batter. She tsked.

"I caught you."

"Then you'd better punish me," he quipped, licking his fingers as he eyed her like she was a chocolate chip. "Melt some chocolate."

"What?"

"Sweetlips, you heard me, melt some chocolate, or better yet, I'll melt some for us," said Foster, a moment before he zapped them to her bedroom.

"We can't."

"Oh yes we can and will," said Foster, forcing Kisha to back up toward the bed.

Kisha fell onto the bed in a heap of giggles. "That's what I love about you, Foster Kane."

"What?" he asked, a devilish grin lighting up his face.

"You've got a sweet tooth," said Kisha, attempting to scramble off the bed.

180

Sweet and Spicy Spells

"You've got no idea," drawled Foster, a second before he zapped them both naked.

"My cookies, they'll burn."

"Sweetlips, the only thing burning is my cock. I'm hot and hard for you."

"Stop that," she admonished.

"Make me," he said, a moment before he drew her already pebbled nipple into his mouth. "That's what I thought, slightly hard. Now, where is that chocolate? Ahh, here it is," he said, drizzling the warm dark liquid onto her nipples.

Kisha groaned loudly, but she was sure the sound was drowned out by Foster's throaty moans as he licked her breasts clean.

"Just like I thought...sweet, so very sweet," muttered Foster, thinking he was the luckiest wizard ever to come across a witch who always smelled like chocolate chip cookies and now even tasted like it. "Heaven, sweet, sweet heaven."

For a wizard who hadn't wanted the assignment, he thanked his brother again and again for that first cut, because otherwise he was sure he'd never have met Kisha Morgan, the sexiest, clumsiest witch in the Northern Hemisphere, whom he loved with a vengeance.

And who would have thought that his brother Zack would fall head over broomstick in love with Prissy. In the last few weeks, Foster realized he no longer thought of Priscilla in the same light. She wasn't cold-hearted or uncaring, that was for sure. He almost laughed at how Priscilla had gotten his brother to ask for her hand in marriage in front of everyone when they finally showed back up to claim her prize for winning the Cauldron Cup.

And who would have thought that he'd learn that he had a younger brother, Josh Neil. Born only eighteen months after him, making Foster the middle child, Josh had become an integral part of their family. Even their mother treated him like

181

one of her own, actually getting mad at Foster when he'd swipe cookies she had specifically made for Josh.

Their mother was an amazing woman, thought Foster. When Magnus told her what happened, she hadn't questioned his loyalty or love. She had simply opened her arms and heart to Josh, treating him like another son. Learning that Josh's mother had attempted to use Josh to get at Magnus tore a hole through his younger brother, but at least he was no longer alone. No, Josh needed a family like every young man. He needed the guidance their father provided him, proud to call him one of his own. Today, in fact, Magnus was legally changing Josh's last name from Neil to Kane, cementing the bond even more.

Foster gulped when he realized his feisty sweetheart of a witch had conjured up cotton candy.

It's good to have a sweet tooth, thought Foster, a moment before the tables were turned and he was lying spread-eagle on the bed, watching as Kisha draped the bright pink candy over the part of him that was standing straight up like a pole.

"It's not fair that you took all the chocolate," she said, licking his cock, sucking the pink cotton candy into her mouth.

Foster felt his balls tighten in sweet anticipation of the game Kisha had given herself up to. He certainly knew exactly where he was going to place that sticky cotton candy once her mouth was full of him.

And that was the way things worked when he and Kisha got together. *Sweets, sweets and more sweets. Just the way I like it.*

Also by Chirstine d'Abo

🔊

eBooks:

Chasing Phoenix

Mistress Rules

No Quarter

Primal Elements

Sweet & Spicy Spells *with Renee Field*

The Bond That Consumes Us

The Bond That Heals Us

The Bond That Saves Us

The Bond That Ties Us

Wizard's Thief

Print Books:

Amethyst Attraction (*anthology*)

The Bond That Heals Us

The Bound that Ties Us

About the Author

෨

It took Christine a lot longer than the average bear to figure out what she wanted to be when she grew up. When she was home on maternity leave, she decided to take a stab at saving her sanity and sat down to write a romance novel. After dabbling with various sub genres she realized she really enjoyed creating strange new worlds and writing about sex. Whether due to the pregnancy hormones or sleep deprivation, she thought this was a great combination.

Many years later her kids are in school and she's back at her day job, but the writing bug is here to stay. When not torturing her characters, she's busy playing with her children or conducting "research" with her husband.

Christine d'Abo welcomes comments from readers. You can find her website and email address on her author bio page at www.ellorascave.com.

Tell Us What You Think

We appreciate hearing reader opinions about our books. You can email us at Comments@EllorasCave.com.

Also by Renee Field

ဆာ

eBooks:
Be My Vampire Tonight
Electrify Me
Elemental Love
Love Me Strong
Love Me Tender
Love Me Wild
Sweet and Spicy Spells *with Christine D'Abo*

Print Books:
Wild and Tender

About the Author

෨

Vivacious by nature, I'm either baking or thinking up my next love scenes—talk about mixing ingredients. Trust me, the recipes are always delicious, especially if chocolate's involved. I juggle writing in between my demanding four children and have discovered some of my best plot themes while driving the mini-van to and from places. I love a good night out on the town where I can discard the mom profile and dance to my heart's content.

Writing has always been my passion. I strongly believe in soulmates and feel eternally lucky that I snatched up mine. The wilder side of me comes out in my erotic writings, where I fuse lustful fantasy with the paranormal edge. I thoroughly enjoy making up worlds, hunky men who cause me to go weak in the knees and intelligent women who can also let their hair down.

Renes Field welcomes comments from readers. You can find her website and email address on her author bio page at www.ellorascave.com.

Tell Us What You Think

We appreciate hearing reader opinions about our books. You can email us at Comments@EllorasCave.com.

Why an electronic book?

We live in the Information Age — an exciting time in the history of human civilization, in which technology rules supreme and continues to progress in leaps and bounds every minute of every day. For a multitude of reasons, more and more avid literary fans are opting to purchase e-books instead of paper books. The question from those not yet initiated into the world of electronic reading is simply: *Why?*

1. *Price.* An electronic title at Ellora's Cave Publishing and Cerridwen Press runs anywhere from 40% to 75% less than the cover price of the exact same title in paperback format. Why? Basic mathematics and cost. It is less expensive to publish an e-book (no paper and printing, no warehousing and shipping) than it is to publish a paperback, so the savings are passed along to the consumer.

2. *Space.* Running out of room in your house for your books? That is one worry you will never have with electronic books. For a low one-time cost, you can purchase a handheld device specifically designed for e-reading. Many e-readers have large, convenient screens for viewing. Better yet, hundreds of titles can be stored within your new library — on a single microchip. There are a variety of e-readers from different manufacturers. You can also read e-books on your PC or laptop computer. (Please note that Ellora's Cave does not endorse any specific brands.

You can check our websites at www.ellorascave.com or www.cerridwenpress.com for information we make available to new consumers.)

3. *Mobility.* Because your new e-library consists of only a microchip within a small, easily transportable e-reader, your entire cache of books can be taken with you wherever you go.

4. *Personal Viewing Preferences.* Are the words you are currently reading too small? Too large? Too… ANNOYING? Paperback books cannot be modified according to personal preferences, but e-books can.

5. *Instant Gratification.* Is it the middle of the night and all the bookstores near you are closed? Are you tired of waiting days, sometimes weeks, for bookstores to ship the novels you bought? Ellora's Cave Publishing sells instantaneous downloads twenty-four hours a day, seven days a week, every day of the year. Our webstore is never closed. Our e-book delivery system is 100% automated, meaning your order is filled as soon as you pay for it.

Those are a few of the top reasons why electronic books are replacing paperbacks for many avid readers.

As always, Ellora's Cave and Cerridwen Press welcome your questions and comments. We invite you to email us at Comments@ellorascave.com or write to us directly at Ellora's Cave Publishing Inc., 1056 Home Avenue, Akron, OH 44310-3502.

Discover for yourself why readers can't get enough of the multiple award-winning publisher
Ellora's Cave.
Whether you prefer e-books or paperbacks,
be sure to visit EC on the web at
www.ellorascave.com
for an erotic reading experience that will leave you breathless.